SANTA'S PUPPY

SANTA'S PUPPY

By Catherine Hapka

Houghton Mifflin Harcourt

BOSTON   NEW YORK

hmhbooks.com

The text was set in Adobe Caslon Pro.
Special thanks to Carrie Garcia, Lauren Litton, and Samoa.
Interior illustrations designed by Ilaria Campana
Designed by Sarah Boecher

The Library of Congress Cataloging-in-Publication data is on file.

ISBN: 978-0-358-05184-8

Printed in the United States of America
DOC 10 9 8 7 6 5 4 3 2 1
4500771643

Christmas Is Coming ...
No, It's Here!

"Hurry, hurry! It's time to go!" the furry white dog barked. He raced across the tundra toward the grazing reindeer. Snow was falling softly and, as usual, the air smelled of gingerbread and pinecones.

One of the reindeer, Vixen, lifted her head. "Keep it down, youngster," she said, peering at the dog. "We're trying to eat, here."

"Right," added her friend Cupid. "We've got a big night coming up, you know."

From the direction of the snow castle on the horizon came the call: "Ahoy, reindeer!" Santa Claus's

jolly voice boomed over the North Pole. "Shake a hoof
—it's almost Christmas! Bring 'em in, Peppermint
Bark!"

"See?" The dog, Peppermint Bark, let his tongue loll
out in a grin. "Told ya so!"

"Fine, fine," the lead reindeer, Dasher, grumbled.
"Let's go, gang."

"This way—follow me!" Peppermint Bark cried,
turning and racing toward Santa with his tail wagging.
Behind him came the thundering sound of hooves, but
a second later there was silence as the reindeer took
flight, soaring over Peppermint Bark's head.

"Go, go!" the young dog barked. "Hurry! It's almost
Christmas!"

An hour later, all eight reindeer were hitched to the
enormous red-and-gold sleigh parked in front of the
North Pole's towering peppermint-striped gates.
Brightly wrapped packages of all shapes and sizes piled
higher and higher in the back as dozens of elves bustled
to and fro, between the sleigh and their workshop. The
elves were dressed in their usual uniform of spruce-

green tunics and red tights, their tiny boots trampling a path through the snow.

"Watch it, short stuff," an elf said, dodging around Peppermint Bark.

"Who you calling short stuff, short stuff?" Peppermint Bark said with a laugh.

Two more elves hurried into view, teetering under the weight of a shiny red bicycle with a bow on the handlebars. "Faster!" the taller elf exclaimed, tugging on her end of the bike. "We have to stay on schedule if Santa is going to leave on time!"

The second elf huffed and puffed. "Sorry, Juniper," he said. "I'll try to do better."

"Can I help?" Peppermint Bark asked Juniper. She had been elected Head Elf this year, and she was taking her job of running and organizing the workshop very seriously.

Juniper rolled her eyes. "Can you help? What do you think?" she said, peering down her long, pointy nose at Peppermint Bark. "It's Christmas! That means all hands on deck."

"All paws on deck too," the second elf, whose name was Happy, added with a chuckle. He blushed. "Er, that was a joke."

Peppermint Bark laughed. "It was funny," he assured his friend. Happy was cheerful and helpful and kind, but he could be a little shy.

Just then several elves rushed over to help wrestle the red bike onto the sleigh, so Peppermint Bark bounded off toward the workshop to look for other ways to help. A package wrapped with a shiny silver ribbon sat just inside. The little white dog carefully grabbed the ribbon in his mouth and carried the gift out to the sleigh.

Santa was there, tying down some packages so they wouldn't fall out when he soared through the sky. "Thanks, buddy," he said, taking the silver-ribboned gift and adding it to the pile. Then the man in red stooped to give Peppermint Bark a rub behind his ears.

"You're welcome." Peppermint Bark swelled with pride knowing that he was Santa's helper, his faithful canine companion, and his best friend. He was the only dog in the world who could say that!

A few minutes later, Peppermint Bark glanced at the clocks built into the front of Santa's snow castle. There were lots of them—one for each time zone on Earth.

The first showed the time on Kiritimati, also known as Christmas Island, and some other islands in the Pacific Ocean. They were in the first time zone to welcome Christmas every year. Right now, that clock stood at five minutes to midnight.

"Ready to go, everyone?" Santa called out.

Juniper stepped forward, her face red with exertion and her striped cap slightly askew. But she looked proud as she saluted.

"The sleigh is loaded and ready to go, Santa," she said. "Right on time!"

"Good job." Santa saluted her back. Then he glanced at the reindeer. "Everyone ready up front?"

"We're ready, Santa," Dasher replied.

The other reindeer nodded. Peppermint Bark leaped forward, wagging his tail.

"I'm ready too, Santa!" he barked. "I want to go with you this year!"

Juniper snorted. "No way. Nobody rides with Santa," she said. "It's just him and the reindeer. Always been that way."

"But why?" Peppermint Bark exclaimed. "I could help, I know I could!"

Santa kneeled down. "Oh, Peppermint Bark," he

said gently. "You're always so helpful around the North Pole—I don't know what I'd do without you to fetch my slippers and keep an eye on the workshop to make sure the elves don't get too distracted playing with the toys they're making . . ." He winked at the elves, who giggled.

"Thanks, Santa." Peppermint Bark felt his heart leap, and he shot Juniper a smug look.

But Santa's next words made the little white pup's whole furry body droop. "However, I'm afraid you'll have to stay home as usual."

"What? Why?" Peppermint Bark cried. "I want to be a *real* Christmas puppy! I want to come with you and see all the children of the world! I know I was still too young last Christmas, but this year . . ."

"I'm sorry, little buddy." Santa patted him. "It's just too risky. If you got out of the sleigh and were left behind—if I couldn't find you before the last time zone strikes midnight . . ."

He glanced toward the huge scrolled gates. Peppermint Bark looked that way too. The gates were tightly shut, just as they remained for 364 days of the year. Only on Christmas did they magically open, allowing Santa to make his special rounds. Every year he and the reindeer flew through the magical portal just outside the gates, which led to other portals all over the globe. The portals allowed Santa to visit every child in the world in a single night. But he had to be very careful to return through the North Pole portal in time, for when the final time zone clicked to one second past midnight on December 26, the gates clanged shut. And nobody—not even Santa—could open them again for the rest of the year.

"But, Santa, I won't leave the sleigh!" Peppermint Bark cried. "I won't! I just want to come with you—I want to help!"

"Thanks, little buddy, but I'm afraid it's not a good idea. Stay here and keep Mrs. Claus company for me, all right?" Santa sounded distracted. He patted his pockets. "Now, where did I put my list?" he muttered.

"Don't forget to check it twice," Peppermint Bark said dejectedly. It was his job to help Santa remember to check his list. And to herd the reindeer. And to make sure the elves kept working, instead of stopping to play with the toys they were making. And even to fetch Santa's slippers when he misplaced them.

The faithful puppy helped with everything else. Why couldn't he help with Santa's Christmas Day deliveries, too? It wasn't fair!

He watched Santa stride off to retrieve his long, long, *long* list of every boy and girl in the world. All the boys and girls Peppermint Bark would never get to see . . . Or would he?

The elves were gathered around Santa as he gave the list one last look. The reindeer were facing the gates, waiting for them to open, already stomping their hooves impatiently. Mrs. Claus was inside the castle. Nobody was looking . . .

This was his chance! Peppermint Bark bounded toward the sleigh. Quick as a wink, he jumped aboard. It felt great to be up there atop the huge pile of gifts!

But he couldn't stay there. If Santa saw him, the man in red would make him stay behind. So Peppermint Bark did what dogs do—he started to dig. He burrowed into the pile, past packages containing trumpets and trampolines and dolls and video games. He dug until only his wagging tail showed, and then he dug down even more . . .

He'd just wriggled into a soft spot between a wrapped cowboy hat and a large teddy bear when he felt the great sleigh start to move. Next came the sound of the enormous gates creaking open. And then Santa's voice rang out: "Ho ho ho—merry Christmas! Let's do this!"

Up on the Wooftop

In a red-shuttered house on a tree-lined block in a pretty little town called Poinsettia, Chris Kerstman peered out the window into the star-spattered midnight sky. "I thought I heard something on the roof," he said.

His sister, Holly, looked up from her book. "Don't be such a baby," she chided. "Santa Claus never comes when kids might actually see him, you know. Ivy says it's been that way since, like, the time of ancient Norse folklore or something."

"Ivy says lots of dumb stuff," Chris muttered. Holly was eleven, just three years older than him, but she acted as if she knew everything and he knew nothing. Especially since this past summer when Ivy Tanaka moved to town. Now that the two girls were best friends, Chris hardly ever saw one without the other.

Having Ivy around ruins everything, Chris thought with a frown. *She'd better not ruin Christmas, too. She might know all about ancient Norse folklore or whatever, but she's got no clue about Christmas in Poinsettia.*

He glanced out the window at the houses across the street. Every last one of them was decorated for the big day. The Garcias had strung blinking red and green lights to make it look as if their house were wrapped in a massive light-up holiday bow. The Fraziers had set up so many inflatable Christmas decorations—a pile of wrapped gifts, a giant Santa-suited penguin, a snow globe with a gingerbread castle inside—that it was hard to see their house at all. And as usual, the Oumas had the biggest, brightest display of all, with the house and shrubs and railings and lampposts twinkling with lights, huge hanging baskets of holly and pine lining the front porch, festive ribbons and balloons like those Mr. Ouma had grown up with in Kenya, and even a life-size light-up Santa, sleigh, and reindeer prancing across the roof.

That was typical for Poinsettia. It was known far

and wide as the Most Christmasy Town in the U.S. of A. The whole place was crazy for Christmas, putting on a month-long holiday market, a huge festival in the town square, a parade with floats and marching bands and live animals, and a contest to choose the year's most festively decorated home and business.

Chris's gaze wandered back inside and over to his sister, who was focused on her book again. If Holly didn't care about trying to catch a glimpse of Santa, why was she staying up until midnight on Christmas Eve, anyway? She even let Chris keep watch from her room, which was the only place in the whole house where you could see the chimney, at least if you leaned out the window and twisted your head around to look straight up . . .

Suddenly Chris sat bolt upright, forgetting his annoyance. Was that the sound of hoofbeats up above? He opened the window and leaned out.

"Hey!" Holly dropped her book and stomped over. "Are you crazy? It's freezing out there! Ivy says she heard it might snow tonight." She slammed the window shut, barely giving her brother a chance to pull his head back in. "You can watch from my window, but you have to keep it closed."

"But I won't be able to see anything that way!" Chris scowled, fed up with his sister's superior attitude. "What's the point?"

Holly put her hands on her hips and glared right back at him. "I don't know," she snapped. "What *is* the point of little brothers? Because I sure can't think of one!"

"Oh yeah?" Chris retorted. "Well, older sisters are the worst idea anyone ever had!" He smirked. "I think Ivy told me that, and she knows everything, right?"

The Kerstman kids' angry voices floated faintly up through the roof into the chilly night air. Santa climbed out of the sleigh, paused, and tilted his head to listen.

"Oh dear," he said. "I thought two good children lived here, but those two don't sound very happy right now."

"Did you double-check your list?" Blitzen the reindeer suggested.

Santa sighed. "No need," he said. "Even good children argue sometimes. Especially brothers and sisters. And especially when they stay up way too late on

Christmas Eve trying to catch a glimpse of you-know-who . . ." With a soft *ho ho ho,* he grabbed two gifts from the sleigh and then disappeared down the chimney.

Deep inside the sleigh, Peppermint Bark stirred in his hiding place. For a while he'd been so excited to be riding in Santa's sleigh that he couldn't think about anything else. But now he realized he couldn't see a thing.

"I'll only stick my head out for a second," he whispered to himself, squeezing past the pointy corners of a board game. "Just long enough to take a quick look around . . ."

Finally he made it to the top of the sleigh. The reindeer were resting and didn't notice him. Santa hadn't yet returned from the chimney.

"Don't be such a dweeb!" a voice rang out from somewhere below.

Peppermint Bark's furry white ears pricked up. What was that? Could it be—a human child? He had never seen one of those before. He'd been born at the North Pole, and he had never set a paw outside the peppermint-striped gates until now.

I have to see one for myself, he thought eagerly. *I have to see one of the creatures that Santa and I and all the others work so hard for all year long! It'll only take a second . . .*

Peppermint Bark jumped down, landing with a soft thump on the shingles. At the front of the sleigh, Comet lifted his head.

"Did you hear that?" he asked.

"I didn't hear anything," his partner, Cupid, replied. "Now, get some rest so I'm not pulling your share by the time we get to Hawaii!"

Ignoring the reindeer's friendly squabbling, Peppermint Bark scurried to the edge of the roof on the far side of the chimney. The voice had come from somewhere down there . . .

He leaned over the edge, peering at the glowing window just below. There! Not one human child, but two! Standing right inside, facing each other. But why did they look so unhappy?

Don't they know it's Christmas? Peppermint Bark thought, leaning even farther down . . .

"Ho ho ho!" a familiar voice rang out from the other side of the chimney. "Shake a hoof, gang! We've got miles to fly before we sleep . . . Merry Christmas, everyone!"

Peppermint Bark spun around at the sound of clattering hooves—followed by silence as the sleigh went airborne. "Wait!" he barked. "I'm still here!"

But it was too late. The reindeer were flying fast, already soaring up, up, up into the night sky . . .

"No!" Santa's puppy yelped, leaping up as if trying to catch them. He was so distracted that he crashed into something solid. "Oof!"

It was the chimney. He grabbed the edge with his front paws and hauled himself up, hoping Santa might glance down and see him there. But Peppermint Bark forgot about the opening.

"Oops!" he cried as he felt himself falling . . .

Do you Hear What I Hear?

Ruff! Arf, arf, woof, woof!

Chris giggled and pulled the lid off the gift box. A cute puppy leaped out and barked again. Ruff! Ruff! There was a bright red bow tied around the puppy's neck, and he ran right over and leaped into Chris's arms, somehow knowing that he belonged to him . . .

Woof!

Chris jerked awake, opening his eyes to the thin rays of early morning sunlight pouring in through his bedroom windows. He sighed. It had been a dream. And not one that was ever going to come true, no matter how hard he wished for it. There wasn't a puppy waiting for him in the pile of gifts under the tree downstairs this Christmas morning. No way. His dad got the nonstop sniffles whenever he was around animals for too long, and that meant none were allowed in the house. Chris had to be satisfied by playing with his friends' pets and walking the Garcias' golden retriever when they went out of town.

Ruff! Ruff!

Chris blinked, wondering if he was still dreaming. Because he would have sworn he'd just heard . . .

"Is that a dog?" Holly barged into his room without knocking, even though she would have yelled at Chris for doing the same thing.

But Chris wasn't focused on that right now. He jumped out of bed. "I heard it too. Where's it coming from?"

His sister tugged on the hem of the oversize basketball jersey she wore as a pajama top. "Outside?" she said, sounding uncertain. "Maybe it's the Garcias' dog."

"Nope. Sounds different." Chris was known as the animal expert in the family, so for once Holly didn't argue with him. "Come on, let's go see what's up."

He kicked on his slippers and rushed downstairs

with Holly on his heels. Their father was in the kitchen fiddling with the coffeemaker.

"Whoa! What's all the commotion, kiddos?" he said, waggling his eyebrows and wearing his patented Dad Smirk. "Hold on . . . Don't tell me — is today some kind of holiday or something? Is that why you two aren't sleeping till noon as usual?"

"It's not that, Dad." Chris hurried past and swung open the back door. A blast of cold wind swept in, along with a few more faint barks from somewhere overhead.

Chris tilted his head, wondering if the wind was messing with his hearing. Because this time, the barks had sounded almost like . . . words. There! He heard the sounds again!

"Did you hear that?" he asked Holly, who had caught up by then. "It sounds like the dog is talking! Like he's saying, *Help, I'm stuck!*"

"Yeah, right, very funny, Doctor Doolittle." Holly rolled her eyes, then shivered and grabbed a parka off the hook near the door. "Brr! Ivy was right — it's freezing out today!"

"Didn't snow overnight, though, did it?" Chris muttered, remembering what his sister had said the night before.

Their father stepped over to join them, his battered old leather slippers flap-flapping on the tiles. "Was that a dog I just heard?" he asked, peering out the door.

Then Chris's mother wandered in, yawning and with her short auburn hair sticking up in tufts. "What's all the racket down here?" she mumbled, heading straight for the coffeemaker. "I was at the hospital late last night. I know it's Christmas morning, but I was hoping to sleep at least until the crack of dawn."

"You put on your lab coat instead of your bathrobe again, Mom," Holly told her with a sigh.

Dr. Kerstman glanced down at herself. "Oops, so I did. Hope I don't wear my robe to the hospital later." She chuckled and grabbed a mug out of the cabinet.

Sometimes Chris was amazed that his mother could be such a good doctor when she could hardly dress herself. Still, he supposed that being able to fix broken bones and stuff was more important than matching socks.

Arf, arf!

Mom's eyes finally opened all the way. "Hey, was that a dog?" she said. "Oh, Chris—you didn't try to sneak in another pet, did you?"

"No, Mom," Chris said, a little sheepish at the

memory of how he'd smuggled a stray kitten into his bedroom the previous summer. Mom had been working double shifts at the hospital that week, and Holly was at sleepaway soccer camp, so it was a while before anyone noticed. Dad had thought he had the world's longest-lasting cold before he finally caught Chris sneaking a couple cans of tuna out of the pantry. Chris's parents had made him give the kitten to one of the nurses at the hospital, who was looking for a new cat.

Ruff, ruff! Help, I'm stuck up here on the roof!

Chris stepped outside. "We have to rescue that dog!" he said. "I think . . . I think he's on the roof."

"How would a dog get on the roof?" Dad stepped outside and looked up. At the next flurry of barks, his eyes widened. "Well, jingle my bells—I think you're right, Chris! It does sound like it's on the roof."

"Maybe it climbed up the cords for the Christmas lights," Holly said. "They're pretty much a huge spider web on the back of the house."

Chris nodded. The Kerstmans weren't likely to win any prizes in the town's best-decorated-home contest this year. Dad had taken on an extra class at the university to cover for a sick colleague that semester, and Mom had been busy at the hospital as usual, which meant there wasn't much time for planning or decorating. So they'd just strung a bunch of multicolored lights on the house and shrubbery and added a few light-up candy canes along the front walk. The cords for all the lights ran down the back of the house to the outdoor outlet, crisscrossing one another and sometimes blocking the windows. Some of the wires were attached to the siding with the peppermint-striped duct tape Dad had bought at the holiday market last year. Others swung freely in any touch of a breeze. It was a mess, but at least the front of the house looked sort of festive.

"Excellent theory, my little Ilex," Mom said with a smile. Ilex was Mom's nickname for Holly—it was the Latin name for the tree she was named after. Mom loved Latin names for things. Probably because that was all they learned in medical school, at least as far as Chris could tell. "But how are we going to get the dog down from up there?" she added.

"I could climb up the cords too," Chris offered.

"What? No!" Mom set her coffee cup down with a clunk, looking alarmed, and joined the others on the back deck. "They'd never hold your weight. And I'll have enough broken bones to set today without adding yours to my workload."

Dad was already heading back inside. "I'll grab the ladder out of the garage."

Five minutes later, the Kerstmans huddled in the backyard, staring up at the roof. Chris had pulled on his sneakers, and his mom had slipped on the clogs she wore to work, but Holly and Dad were still in their slippers. Holly hopped from foot to foot, shivering dramatically. "This is crazy," she said. "It's freezing out here! I'm going back inside."

But she didn't. She just pulled her hands into the sleeves of her parka like a turtle pulling its head into its shell, watching as Dad leaned the ladder against the gutter near the chimney.

Woof! Help me, please!

"He sounds scared." Chris peered upward. He could barely see the top of the chimney. "Hold on, doggy!" he called out. "We're coming!"

Arf! Okay! But hurry, it's dark in here!

Dark? Chris squinted up at the winter sun. What did the dog mean by that?

Mom was watching Dad adjust the ladder. "Watch out for the cords," she said. "We really should have braided them or something."

Dad glanced upward. "I'm trying to get close to the chimney—sounds like the dog might be stuck in there."

Holly blinked. "In the *chimney?*" she said. "How in the world would a dog get in there?"

"No, I think he's right," Chris blurted out, finally understanding the "dark in here" thing.

"Maybe it's Santa Dog, and he got stuck trying to deliver our presents," Dad said with a chuckle, settling the ladder against the edge of the roof. "Now, who wants to climb up there?"

"Me!" Chris said, stepping forward.

His mother pulled him back with a hand on his shoulder. "You do it, Kenny," she told Dad. "You managed not to fracture your fibula putting the lights up, right?"

"That's confidence, Mom," Holly said with a snort. "I don't think any of us should go up there. Maybe we can just call the town dogcatcher or something."

Dad smiled at her. "I'm not sure Poinsettia has a dogcatcher, sweetie," he said. "Anyway, I'll be fine. If I fall off and break my legs, your mother can put me back together. Right, honey?"

"I'm not on duty until noon," Mom said with a

shrug. "But I'm sure someone can slap on a couple of casts in the ER."

"Very funny." Dad took a deep breath, then grabbed the ladder.

Chris held his breath as his father started to climb —one rung, two, three . . . Then Chris looked up at the chimney—what he could see of it from here, anyway. Was there really a dog inside? How had it even . . .

Suddenly he heard a funny little ripping sound. He glanced toward his father, who was halfway up the ladder. Chris's eyes widened.

"Watch it, Dad," he called. "The back of your slipper is caught in one of the cords!"

"Huh?" Dad paused with his left foot halfway to the next rung. A green power cord dangled off the heel of his slipper with a strip of colorful duct tape still attached.

"He's right, Kenny," Mom said. "Shake it loose, or you'll bring the lights down on your head."

Dad nodded and shook his foot—so vigorously that both cord and slipper went flying!

"Oops," he said. He put his bare foot down on the next rung, then yanked it back again just as quickly. "Yow!" he cried. "That's cold!"

"Daddy!" Holly exclaimed. "Be careful, you're tipping!"

"Come back down," Mom added. "You can put on your shoes and try again."

Dad set his bare left foot down again, gingerly this time, his knobby toes curling around the rung. "Coming," he said.

Just then came the faint sound of a tinny, twinkly version of "Jingle Bell Rock." "Sounds like the Fraziers turned on their singing snow globe," Holly muttered.

Up on the ladder, Dad started humming along. "I love this song," he said, nodding his head to the beat.

Meanwhile he fished for the lower rung with his right foot—the one that still had a slipper on it. But he was distracted by the music, and his foot went too far forward. When he tried to yank it back, the back of the slipper got caught on the rung.

"Yikes!" Dad exclaimed as his foot slipped forward . . .

"Kenny!" Mom cried.

"Dad!" Chris yelped, as Holly let out a little scream.

"Aaaahh!" Dad blurted out as he lost his grip on the ladder and fell backwards . . .

Chris squeezed his eyes shut, visions of his father

landing headfirst on the hard, frozen ground flashing through his mind. At least Mom would know what to do . . .

But when Chris cracked one eye open, hardly daring to look, he saw that his father hadn't fallen after all. His right leg was hooked over a rung of the ladder—leaving him dangling upside down a yard above the ground!

"A little help here, guys?" Upside-Down Dad said with a sigh.

Arf, arf! Is anyone coming?

Chris looked up and gulped. The dog's barks sounded weaker. How long had he been up there?

"We need to get the dog out of there before . . ." Chris began anxiously.

Mom silenced him with a look. "We'll rescue the dog," she said. "First, though, we need to rescue your father."

Before long, Dad was safely back on the ground. Holly helped him dig his left slipper out of the bushes while Mom moved the ladder over a few feet.

"Can I climb up this time?" Chris asked as he helped her.

"Absolutely not," she replied. "And your father's not going again either."

Holly heard her and looked over. "I hope you don't think *I'm* climbing up on the roof to rescue some random stray dog," she said. "That's not exactly how I planned to spend Christmas morning."

Chris glared at her. She really *had* changed. The old Holly had always been ready for an adventure. How many hours had the two of them spent catching tadpoles in the stream in the town park? How many nights had they stayed up late telling each other spooky stories by flashlight in the backyard tent? Or kept each other awake to wait up for Santa, or . . . ?

"You're not going up either," Mom told Holly, breaking into Chris's thoughts. "I'll go."

She grabbed the sides of the ladder and stepped onto the first rung. Chris hurried over to hold one side of the ladder, while his father steadied the other side.

"Be careful, honey," Dad said.

"I was born careful." Mom climbed steadily upward, her lab coat flapping in the cold breeze.

Ruff, ruff!

Chris held his breath, standing on tiptoes to peer up at his mother as she crawled onto the roof. She stood up gingerly beside the chimney and peered inside.

"Is the dog in there?" he called.

Mom reached down into the chimney . . . and pulled out a fluffy, wiggly, soot-covered little creature! He was about the size of a large raccoon but furrier, with a fluffy, wagging tail.

"Got him!" she called. "Hold the ladder—we're coming down."

4

A Christmas Tail

Peppermint Bark sucked in a deep breath of fresh air. Whew! It felt as if he'd been stuck in that sooty chimney forever! He tried not to wiggle too much as the human woman clutched him close and climbed down the ladder.

But once they were on the ground, he couldn't hold back any longer. The moment the woman set him down, Peppermint Bark erupted into a whirlwind of jumping and leaping and joyful barking.

"Thank you, thank you!" he barked, his tail wagging nonstop as he tried to lick anyone he could reach.

The girl squealed and pushed him away when he

jumped up against her legs, but the smaller human child —the boy with the tousled sandy hair and wide brown eyes—kneeled down and hugged Peppermint Bark.

"You're welcome," the human child said. "How'd you get stuck in there, anyway?"

"Long story," Peppermint Bark told him.

"Oh, okay," the child said. "Maybe you can tell me about it later."

The human man chuckled. "Talking to animals, just like always, eh, Chris?" he said in a joking tone.

Peppermint Bark tilted his head curiously. "What do you mean?" he barked at the man.

But the man turned away without answering to say something to the woman. For a second Peppermint Bark was confused. He could tell the boy understood him. But he realized the other humans hadn't responded to anything he'd said. Couldn't they hear his words?

"I'm Chris," the boy said. "What's your name?"

"Peppermint Bark," the little dog replied.

Chris couldn't stop petting and staring at the shaggy, dirty, but still adorable half-grown puppy—Peppermint Bark. That was his name. And Chris knew that because the little dog had just *told* him.

Was he still asleep and dreaming? Because Chris had never heard of a talking dog. And that wasn't the only way Peppermint Bark was different from any other dog Chris had ever seen. His breath smelled like peppermint and hot cocoa and freshly fallen snow. And every time he wagged his tail, there was the faint sound of jingle bells . . .

"Can we go back inside now?" Holly complained. "I'm freezing my toes off!"

"Don't do that, my little frozen Ilex," Mom said with a chuckle. "If your toes fall off, you'll have to go to the hospital to have them sewn back on. And the emergency room is always packed on Christmas. That's why I have to go in for a few hours later today, remember?"

Chris remembered. He remembered lots of holidays when his mom had to work. It was great that she was such a good doctor that everyone needed her to take care of their busted ankles and cracked ribs. But did she really have to work on Christmas?

"Right." Dad chuckled. He picked up the ladder and headed for the garage. "Plus all those candy cane overdoses and paper cuts from opening gifts . . ."

"Come on, Peppermint Bark," Chris said to the little dog, not wanting to think about Mom's job anymore. "Let's go inside and warm up."

"Sure—thanks!" Peppermint Bark frolicked ahead toward the back door, following Mom. "But it's already really warm here, at least compared to back home! And hey, where's all the snow?"

Meanwhile Holly shot Chris a funny look. "What did you call him?" she asked.

"Peppermint Bark," Chris said. "That's his name."

His sister rolled her eyes. "Okay, whatever. I would've named him Pigpen myself—look how dirty he is."

Just then Mom let out a shout. "Somebody stop that filthy little beast! He's leaving tracks everywhere!"

Chris dashed forward. But it was too late. Peppermint Bark had already raced in excited circles around the kitchen, leaving sooty paw prints all over the white tile floor.

"This is amazing!" the little dog barked. "The floor is slippery like ice, but it's warm!"

"Stop!" Chris cried. "You're all dirty from being in the chimney!"

Peppermint Bark skidded to a halt, tilting his head

to look up at him. "Sorry, Chris," he said. "I didn't mean to make a mess."

"It's okay," Chris told him.

Holly was glancing around the kitchen with a frown. "It's *not* okay," she said. "I don't feel like mopping the floor on Christmas morning, do you?"

For a second, Chris thought she'd actually heard the dog's words. "He already apologized," he said. "You don't have to make him feel bad."

Holly stared at him. "Grow up," she snapped. "You're too old to pretend to talk to animals. It was bad enough when you were five and pretended your goofy stuffed tiger was your best friend."

Chris glared back at her. Why was she always saying things like that? He felt like reminding her that she'd had a favorite stuffed animal too—Rufus the elephant. Chris had helped Dad pick out the plush pachyderm for Holly's sixth birthday . . . But what was the point in thinking about stuff like that? She wasn't the old Holly anymore. That Holly was gone, and there was nothing Chris could do to get her back.

Dad was already wiping the floor with a rag, while Mom pulled the broom out of a closet, looking slightly annoyed. Chris quickly picked up Peppermint Bark. He was heavier than he looked, but Chris hardly noticed. "I'll give him a bath, okay?" he said. "Then I'll help you guys clean the kitchen."

His father looked up and nodded. "Thanks, son."

"Try not to make too much of a mess in the bathtub," Mom added.

"Okay." Chris held Peppermint Bark tightly, hurrying toward the stairs before his parents could change their minds.

The furry pup snuggled against him, breathing peppermint and chocolate into his face. "Thanks, Chris."

"You're welcome," Chris whispered, shooting a glance over his shoulder to make sure Holly wasn't listening.

Upstairs, Chris filled the tub with warm water. He added some flower-scented bubbles, even though they were Holly's and she'd probably be mad.

"Okay, hop in," he told the little dog. "I'll scrub the soot off you."

"Thanks." Peppermint Bark jumped into the tub with a splash. The water darkened immediately as the soot started coming off. "It's nice and warm—just the same temperature Mrs. Claus always makes my baths."

Chris blinked. "Mrs. Claus?" he echoed. "Is that your owner?"

Peppermint Bark shook his head to get a soap bubble off his nose, which made his ears flap. "Well, technically I'm Santa's puppy," he said. "But Mrs. Claus is his wife, so . . ."

"Hold on a sec." Chris sat back on his heels, forgetting all about scrubbing. "Santa? As in, Santa Claus? White beard, red suit?"

"That's the guy." The little dog—more white than soot-colored by now—turned his tail toward Chris. "Could you scratch my backside? It's a little itchy—I think I got extra dirty back there."

Chris obeyed, his head spinning with what Peppermint Bark had just told him. "Santa Claus . . ." he murmured. "You're Santa's puppy! No wonder you can talk!"

The dog turned to face him again. "Yeah, what's up with that?" he said. "Your family acted like they didn't hear anything I said." He tilted his head, peering at Chris quizzically. "And now that I think about it, you acted like you'd never heard a dog talk before."

"That's because dogs *don't* talk," Chris replied. "At least not any that I ever met before."

"Oh." Peppermint Bark thought about that for a second. "Maybe it's a North Pole thing. Santa says lots of stuff is different up there than it is here. Like, we don't have cars or the flu or mosquitoes. And we do have elves, and flying reindeer . . ."

"Yeah." Chris smiled. "Definitely different."

"Okay. But that still doesn't explain why your family can't hear me," Peppermint Bark went on. "Santa says anyone with enough Christmas spirit can see him and the reindeer if that person looks at just the right time. It probably works the same for hearing me talk, since that's just another part of Christmas magic."

"That's probably it, then." Chris's shoulders slumped. "Holly doesn't have much Christmas spirit these days. And my parents are both pretty busy—maybe they don't either."

"Wow." Peppermint Bark's eyes widened. "That's so sad! Maybe I can help."

Chris brightened. Did Peppermint Bark really think he could help the Kerstmans regain their Christmas spirit?

Why not? Chris told himself. *He's Santa's puppy, after all . . .*

Peppermint Bark ducked his head under the water and came up blowing bubbles. "This is fun!" he said.

"At first I was really scared when I got left behind. But the rest of the world is super interesting! I found out there's no snow here, and chimneys are really dark, and people sing a lot less than elves do . . ." He wagged his tail, sending more soap bubbles flying.

"Wait—you were left behind?" Chris grabbed a towel to mop up the mess the bubbles were leaving on the floor. "What do you mean?"

"That's why I'm here." Peppermint Bark looked up. "See, I'm not technically allowed to ride along with Santa on his Christmas deliveries. Nobody rides with him—it's just him and the reindeer. Always been that way."

"So what happened?" Chris asked.

Peppermint Bark dipped his head, looking sheepish. "I sort of . . . um . . . stowed away. And when Santa stopped here, I got out of the sleigh to look around, and, well . . ."

"He left without you." Chris grabbed another fresh towel. "I think you're pretty clean—come on out and dry off."

"Okay." Peppermint Bark hopped out of the tub . . . and shook himself, sending water and bubbles everywhere!

"Oh no!" Chris yelped, throwing the towel over the little dog.

But it was too late. The floor was dotted with puddles. Streaks of foamy soap bubbles dripped down the mirror. Even the curtains had little damp spots.

Peppermint Bark peeked out from under the towel. "Sorry, Chris," he said meekly. "Did I mess up again?"

"No, it's okay," Chris said quickly. "You didn't mess up. But here—I'll finish drying you with the towel, okay?"

"Thanks, Chris."

Chris rubbed the little dog dry. It was pretty steamy in the bathroom, but that wasn't the only reason Chris suddenly felt warm all over. He could hardly believe Santa's puppy was right here in his house, talking to him. Already feeling like a new friend.

"There! You're pretty dry," Chris said after a moment. He tossed the towel into the hamper and smiled at Peppermint Bark. The damp little dog gazed back at him happily. His pink tongue lolled out of his mouth, and his big brown eyes sparkled like twinkling Christmas lights . . .

"Chris!" Mom's voice floated up from downstairs. "Is that dog clean yet? Because we need to talk."

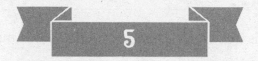

5

Who'll Be Home for Christmas?

When Chris and Peppermint Bark got downstairs, the others were sitting in the living room—Mom and Dad on the sofa, and Holly in her favorite overstuffed chair. Someone had plugged in the Christmas tree, and it glimmered and glowed in front of the bay window.

"Great tree!" Peppermint Bark barked.

"Thanks," Chris whispered. But he was distracted. Mom and Dad had serious looks on their faces.

He glanced at his sister for a hint at what was up. But Holly wasn't paying attention. She was staring at the piles of gifts under the tree. Suddenly she leaned over and grabbed a small silver-and-red present.

"Is this it?" she demanded eagerly. "Did you guys get me the necklace?"

"Holly, hush," Mom said. "We'll get to the gifts in a moment. First we need to figure out what to do with the dog." Her gaze wandered to Peppermint Bark. "At least he's clean now . . ."

"What do you mean, what to do with him?" Chris glanced down at Peppermint Bark, who was still staring happily at the tree.

Mom and Dad traded a look. "You know he can't stay here, son," Dad said. "With my allergies . . ."

"Okay, yeah, I know." Chris's heart sank. They couldn't be talking about sending Peppermint Bark away already! He'd just arrived! "But we can try to, um, find his owner, right?"

"There's an animal shelter over in Westfield," Dad said. "If he's lost, his owner will probably look for him there."

Not if his owner is Santa Claus, Chris thought.

Holly looked up, finally tuning in to the conversation. "Wait—we're not driving all the way to Westfield now, are we?" she demanded. "Ivy will be here soon! I told her we'd start opening gifts and stuff around nine."

"No, we can't take him in today," Mom told her. "The shelter's closed on Christmas Day—I just checked the website. We'll have to go tomorrow."

For a second Chris was relieved. Peppermint Bark didn't have to leave yet! And tomorrow was a whole day away. Maybe by then Chris could convince his parents to let the little dog stay longer . . .

Then he realized what his sister had said. "Ivy?" he said with a frown. "It's Christmas—can't you live without her for one day?"

Holly frowned back. "Don't you listen to anything I say?" she exclaimed. "Her family doesn't do Christmas, so I invited her to come over. Mom and Dad said it was okay."

"The more the merrier," Dad agreed with a chuckle.

Chris just shrugged. Now he did remember—but that didn't mean he had to like it.

Mom glanced at her watch. "Is it really almost nine already? We'd better get cracking—I need to leave for the hospital by eleven thirty at the latest." She jumped to her feet. "Get dressed, everyone. Back down here in ten minutes for breakfast."

"But can't we open one present first?" Holly said, still clutching the small package. "Please?"

"Yeah." Chris reached for a present with his name on it. "Just one won't hurt, right?"

Dad plucked the gift out of his hand. "You sound like my students begging for one more week to finish their term papers," he said with a wink. "Upstairs. Gifts *after* clothes and breakfast."

Holly rolled her eyes at Chris. He smiled, remembering lots of other Christmases when the two of them had joined forces to convince their parents to let them open a gift or two before breakfast. Maybe the old Holly wasn't totally gone after all—maybe her Christmas spirit was coming back . . .

Then she tossed her gift back under the tree. "I guess you're right," she told their parents. "Like I said, Ivy will be here soon. We don't want to scare her off by forcing her to see Dad in his ratty old pajamas, right?"

"Right," Chris muttered, his hope fading. "We definitely don't want that."

He stomped upstairs with Peppermint Bark hurrying after him. It was bad enough that Mom and Dad would both be gone for half of Christmas Day. Mom would be at work, of course, and Dad had to set up for tonight's town festival and parade. He had spent his winter break this year working on the planning committee. Now Chris had to share the short time he had with his parents with dumb old Ivy, too?

As soon as he and Peppermint Bark were in his room, Chris slammed the door. The puppy jumped at the noise.

"What's the matter?" Peppermint Bark asked. "You shouldn't be in a bad mood—it's Christmas!"

"I know," Chris muttered. "Too bad my annoying sister doesn't know what that means anymore."

He stomped over to grab the sweatshirt he'd left draped on a chair the night before. Peppermint Bark trotted after him.

"Why do you say that?" the little dog asked curiously. "And hey, who's Ivy?"

"She's my weird sister's weird best friend," Chris said. "Her parents grew up in Japan, and they don't really celebrate Christmas in the same way there. That's why Holly invited her over."

Now he remembered Holly telling them all about it. How Ivy's parents had moved to the United States just a couple of years before she was born. How they'd always visited relatives back in Japan or taken other vacations during this time of year, since they were both professors at Poinsettia Valley University like Chris's dad and had time off. How they couldn't go anywhere this year because Ivy's mom was busy writing a book, and so Ivy didn't have anything special to do, and she'd always been interested in learning more about Christmas folklore and traditions and stuff. Somehow, though, it hadn't really dawned on Chris until now what it meant.

"Christmas is supposed to be for family!" he blurted out with a scowl.

Peppermint Bark stood on his hind legs and licked Chris's hand, sending the scent of peppermint wafting through the air. "Friends can be family too," the puppy said. "That's what Santa says. He says we're all one big North Pole family—him and Mrs. Claus and the elves and the reindeer and me . . ." He looked sad for a second.

That made Chris forget about his own problems. Somehow, in all the excitement of finding Peppermint Bark, he hadn't really thought about how the little dog must feel. Lost, far away from home on Christmas . . .

"Don't worry," Chris said. "I'll help you figure out how to get home."

Peppermint Bark brightened immediately. "Really?" he barked. "You'd do that? But you've helped me so much already—rescuing me from the chimney, giving me that wonderful bath . . ." He leaped around happily, almost knocking over the Good Sport trophy Chris had won at day camp this past summer. Holly always made fun of that trophy, since she'd won the Most Valuable Player trophy for three different sports at the same camp. But Chris didn't care what she thought.

Chris caught the trophy and set it on a higher shelf. "Of course I'll help you," he told Peppermint Bark. "You're my friend. And that makes you family. At least that's what Santa always says, right?"

He quickly pulled on his clothes. Then he and Peppermint Bark ran back downstairs.

When they got there, Ivy was just stepping in through the front door. She carried a small stack of wrapped gifts, and her cheeks were pink from the cold.

"Welcome, Ivy," Dad said. "Come on in—can I make you a smoothie, or would you rather have toast and jam? Holly talked me out of making pancakes since we're short of time this morning."

"Yeah." Holly glanced at Peppermint Bark. "We got a little, um, delayed."

"A smoothie sounds great, thanks," Ivy said politely. Ivy was always polite, at least when adults were around. She didn't talk to Chris much at all otherwise.

Peppermint Bark trotted over to the visitor, his tail wagging. Ivy took a step backwards, looking startled.

"You got a dog?" she said.

"Not exactly," Mom said with a chuckle. "More like, this dog got us."

Ivy wrinkled her nose, ducking behind Holly. "Sorry, I'm a little sensitive to bad smells," she said.

"Bad smells?" Chris protested, insulted on Peppermint Bark's behalf. "He just had a bath."

Ivy shrugged. "Like I said, I'm sensitive." She tucked a strand of her straight black hair behind one ear. "Maybe you could keep him a little ways away?"

"Sure, of course." Holly nudged Peppermint Bark with one foot. "We can lock him in another room or something."

"No way!" Chris protested. "Peppermint Bark is part of this family too." Noticing his parents' surprised looks, he added, "At least for today."

"That's his name?" Ivy peered around Holly, looking curious. "Peppermint Bark? Cute."

"That's me!" the little dog barked. "Nice to meet you, Ivy."

Suddenly Ivy's eyes went very wide. "Did you—did he just . . ." she stammered uncertainly.

"What?" Chris demanded. He was suddenly extremely interested in what Ivy was about to say—maybe for the first time ever . . .

Holly was glad that Ivy was finally here. So far, Christmas morning had mostly been a lot of standing around with cold toes, thanks to that scruffy puppy. Sure, he was cute, sort of like a snow-white version of Benji or something, but what was the point of getting attached? Dad's allergies meant he couldn't stay, and that was that.

And it didn't help that her little brother was acting like even more of a weirdo than usual. How old did that kid have to get before he stopped believing that animals could talk?

"Just get in here, okay?" Holly said, grabbing Ivy by the arm and dragging her toward the living room before she could finish whatever she was saying. "I'm dying to open gifts! I'm expecting something very special this year . . ." She shot her parents a hopeful look. Had they given her the amazing birthstone necklace she'd asked for? The one that was made of real gold, and that matched Ivy's except for the color of the stone—purple amethyst for Ivy, blue sapphire for Holly? The one she'd been drooling over all year?

"Breakfast first, then gifts," Mom said. "Into the kitchen, everyone."

Dad was a pretty good cook, but he could be slow. Holly didn't have time for that today. "I'll help cut stuff up," she offered. "You can help too, Ives."

"What?" Ivy was looking over her shoulder at the dog. She blinked and glanced at Holly. "Oh—I mean, sure, I'd love to help."

With Holly and Ivy assisting, it didn't take long for Dad to make breakfast smoothies for everyone. He even mixed up some chicken soup and peanut butter to make one for Peppermint Bark.

"Let's see if this pup knows any tricks," Dad said, pouring the dog's smoothie into a bowl. "Sit, Peppermint Bark! If you do, you get a treat!"

Peppermint Bark barked and sat down. Chris gave him a pat.

"Good job, buddy," he said. "Hold on, Dad—I bet I can teach him a better trick. Hey, Peppermint Bark, please fetch me that dishtowel! The one with the Christmas wreaths on it."

"Enough already," Holly complained. She'd already sucked down half her berry banana smoothie, while her brother hadn't even started his.

But her eyes widened when the little dog trotted over to the wreath-patterned dishtowel hanging near the sink. He grabbed it in his mouth and brought it back to Chris, tail wagging the whole time.

"Whoa." Ivy looked impressed. "That was cool! How'd you know he could do that?"

Chris smirked in that annoying way he had whenever he thought he was being smarter than everyone else—in other words, most of the time. "Just a lucky guess," he said as their father set the bowl in front of Peppermint Bark.

Holly rolled her eyes. She was getting tired of Chris hogging all the attention with that silly dog. Why bother teaching him tricks and acting all lovey-dovey when he'd be leaving tomorrow?

She sucked down the last few drops of her smoothie. "Finish up, guys," she said. "Those gifts aren't going to open themselves!"

Peppermint Bark loved watching the humans perform their Christmas morning rituals. It was all so interesting! Santa had taught him a lot about the various things people did to celebrate the big day—gifts, caroling, Christmas trees, and much more. But Santa had never even mentioned Christmas morning smoothies.

"You got it for me!" Holly squealed, startling Peppermint Bark out of his thoughts. She dug into the small box she'd just unwrapped. Then she held up something thin and sparkly. "Oh, you guys, I love it! Thank you so much!"

Ivy gasped. "You got the necklace!" she cried. She pulled a similar sparkly strand from beneath the collar of her shirt. "Just like mine!"

Peppermint Bark had seen the elves make sparkly necklaces lots of times. He wasn't sure why they meant so much to humans. But he could tell that Holly was happy—just like everyone should be on Christmas.

"Merry Christmas!" he barked gleefully, wagging his tail and rushing closer.

Ivy spun to face him, her eyes wide. Peppermint Bark tilted his head to one side, noticing the surprised look on her face.

"Can you understand what I'm saying?" he barked at her curiously.

Instead of answering, Ivy shrank back into her chair and glanced over at Holly. "Um, that dog is stepping on the gifts."

Holly glanced up from studying her necklace. "Hey, shoo, fuzz face." She pushed Peppermint Bark off a large present.

Peppermint Bark moved over to a bare spot on the rug. Suddenly he smelled something familiar. Pine-cones and gingerbread—just like home!

"A portal!" he barked, homesickness and excitement washing over him in equal measure. "I smell a portal! Where is it?"

"What's wrong with him?" Ivy asked, staring at the dog with that same expression of surprise.

But this time Peppermint Bark didn't notice. He started pawing at the stack of gifts nearby, searching for the one hiding the portal back home.

"There it is!" he barked as he found the box with the North Pole smell. The portal had to be inside! "I'm coming, Santa!" he cried, shredding paper and ribbon as fast as he could.

6

No Time Like the Present

"Hey!" Dad shouted. "The dog is attacking the gifts!"

Chris jumped forward, confused. Peppermint Bark was barking nonstop, so frantic that his words were a jumble. The only ones Chris could understand were "smell," "Santa," and "portal"—whatever that last one meant.

"He's probably just, um, excited," Chris told his family. He grabbed Peppermint Bark around the middle and lifted him off the package, which was a shredded mess by now. The little dog's legs windmilled wildly in midair as he tried to wiggle free.

"Put me down, Chris!" Peppermint Bark cried. "Please! I need to uncover the portal before it closes!"

Holly darted forward to grab the shredded gift. "Who was this for?" she asked, pulling something out of the scraps of wrapping paper and ribbon. "It's a scented candle."

"That's for your mother, from me," Dad said. He chuckled. "I hope she likes the smell better than the dog seems to . . ."

Chris was hugging Peppermint Bark tighter. "Listen," he whispered into the puppy's white ear. "You have to settle down, or they'll lock you in another room!"

Peppermint Bark abruptly stopped struggling. He stared at the candle as Holly handed it to Mom. "A scented candle?" he whimpered. "That's what I smelled?"

Mom was examining the candle, which was encased in a glass jar and seemed unharmed. "What was that all about?" She glanced at Dad. "I'm starting to wonder if it's a good idea to let a strange dog stay here when we're both gone, Kenny. What if he tries to eat the house? Or the kids?"

"He won't," Chris promised quickly. "I'll keep him under control. I swear."

He set Peppermint Bark on the floor at his feet. The little dog trotted over to Mom and licked her hand. "I'm sorry," he barked softly.

"Don't worry—I'm in charge while you're both gone, right?" Holly shot Chris a sour look. "If the dog causes any trouble, I'll lock him in the garage or something."

Chris frowned at her. "Why is she in charge?"

"Because I'm older, that's why," Holly said, as if it were the most obvious thing in the world. "It's not like I *want* to babysit you, okay? Especially on Christmas."

Dad looked worried. "Maybe I should stay home after all, keep an eye on things . . ."

"You can't," Mom told him. "If you don't show up for your shift at the square, we'll never hear the end of it from Mr. Brooks."

She and Dad both rolled their eyes. Chris did too. Mr. Brooks wasn't actually the mayor of Poinsettia, but just about everyone thought he acted like it. He'd lived there in his big old Victorian house at the edge of Poinsettia Square for his entire seventy-three years of life, and he seemed to think that gave him a right to boss everyone else around. He'd been the president of the

Poinsettia Holiday Festival Committee for longer than Chris had been alive.

"I suppose you're right." Dad still looked concerned, but he shrugged. "Anyway, the kids will only be on their own for a few hours before the festival starts. And Ivy's parents are just a block away if there's any trouble. Right, Ivy?"

"That's right, Mr. Kerstman," Ivy said politely. "My mom said we should call if we need them."

"Good, good." Mom glanced at her watch. "Let's keep going, then. Lots of gifts still to open, hmm?"

Peppermint Bark had backed away and was sitting quietly at Chris's feet. Chris let out the breath he hadn't even realized he was holding. That was the good part about Mom being so scatterbrained about everything but work: sometimes she forgot she was mad about something.

"Here, Dad," Chris said, grabbing a bright red-and-gold package from the pile still under the tree. "This one's from me. I hope you like it."

Dad ripped the paper off to reveal a long, narrow box. "Hmm, what could it be? Maybe a big-screen TV?" he joked, shaking the box. "Or a pair of snowshoes? I know—a new battery for my car!"

Ivy giggled. "Very funny, Mr. K!"

Peppermint Bark wagged his tail. "Yeah, your dad's funny," he told Chris. "I know an elf like that—his name's Happy because he's always cracking silly jokes and making everyone laugh."

Chris noticed that Ivy had spun in her seat to stare at the little dog again. Had she understood his words?

No way, Chris thought. *Becoming best friends with Ivy is the whole reason Holly got so weird and lost her Christmas spirit—Ivy definitely can't hear Peppermint Bark if my own sister and parents can't!*

Dad finally opened the box. Inside, nestled among layers of tissue paper, was a tie with candy canes printed all over it. He held it up with a grin.

"I love it!" he exclaimed. "It'll go perfectly with my Santa-print belt. Thanks, son."

"You're welcome," Chris said. "Okay, Mom, here's one for you . . ."

Peppermint Bark wasn't sure how much longer the family spent opening their gifts. He loved watching every second of it. Each member of the family had given the others thoughtful, special presents. Chris received some action figures, a board game, books, and new sneakers. In addition to her sparkly necklace, Holly got a nice tennis racket, a new case for her cell phone, several books, and lots of clothes. Dad got a new banjo, which he tested out by playing some Christmas carols. Mom got jewelry from Dad and a birdbath for the backyard from the kids. Faraway relatives had sent gifts for everyone, and a few neighbors had dropped off packages containing home-baked cookies or other items. Santa had contributed a pretty purple bike helmet for Holly and a cute stuffed owl for Chris.

There were gifts for Ivy, too — a hand-beaded bracelet from Holly, a book about local folklore from Dad, and a wool scarf embroidered with ivy vines from Mom. Even Chris had given her a fancy bookmark.

"Mom and Dad told me I had to get her something, since she was coming over for Christmas," he whispered to Peppermint Bark. "They paid for it, though."

Peppermint Bark tilted his head to look up at the boy. Sometimes the little dog didn't quite understand what Chris was talking about.

"What do you mean?" he barked.

Holly looked up from admiring her birthstone necklace. "Does he have to bark so much?" she complained. "I'm trying to enjoy Christmas."

Mom stood up. "I hate to put an end to the fun," she said, "but I need to get to work. Come on, Kenny—I'll drop you off at the square on my way to the hospital."

Beside him, Peppermint Bark could sense Chris stiffening. "You have to go already?" Chris said.

"Sorry, kiddo, duty calls." Dad ruffled Chris's hair. "We'll see you later at the festival, though, right? You can walk over with Ivy's folks or other neighbors if you don't want to go by yourselves."

Mom was already grabbing her purse. "Right. Stay in the house until then. It's too cold to play outside today anyway."

"Sure, no problem," Holly said. She'd already snapped the new cover onto her phone, which she was using to take selfies of herself and Ivy posing with their matching necklaces. "See you later."

🎄

Chris stood on the front porch and waved as the car pulled out of the driveway. Dad waved back, though Mom was focused on her driving and didn't see him.

"Shut the door!" Holly shouted from somewhere inside. "You're letting all the cold air in!"

Chris frowned, tempted to leave the door standing open just to prove that his sister couldn't order him around—even if she *thought* she was in charge.

But it really was pretty cold, so he closed the door behind him when he stepped inside. Then he and Peppermint Bark went back into the living room. The girls had disappeared, though Chris could hear them giggling and talking in the kitchen.

The living room was a mess, with gifts sitting around on every surface and scraps of ribbon and colorful wrapping paper all over the floor. Chris picked up his stuffed owl and studied it, trying to decide what its name should be. Owlie? Wise Guy? Feathers? Then he noticed Mom's new scented candle nearby.

"Hey," he said to Peppermint Bark, who was sniffing at the tinsel on the tree. "What was that all about earlier? You know—attacking that candle like you did?"

"Sorry about that, Chris." The puppy's tail drooped. "It smelled like home, so I thought it was a portal leading back to the North Pole."

"A portal?" Chris remembered hearing that word in the dog's flurry of excited barks. "What's that?"

Peppermint Bark looked uncertain. "It's like a magical gate, I think?" he said. "Or maybe more like a tunnel. Anyway, there's a big one back home—Santa and the reindeer fly through it to get here." He looked around. "To the rest of the world, I mean. Santa says there are lots of portals all over the planet to help him get everywhere he needs to go on Christmas Day."

"But what do they look like?" Chris glanced again at the scented candle. "Wouldn't a portal have to be a lot bigger than a candle if a whole sleigh is going to fly through it?"

Peppermint Bark sighed. "I'm not sure," he said. "All I know is that they smell like the North Pole —and they're disguised so people can't stumble into one." He looked up at Chris with sad brown eyes. "But I need to find one if I'm ever going to get home again."

Before Chris could respond, Ivy burst into the room. "Hey!" she shouted, scowling at Chris with her hands on her hips. "I'm getting really freaked out here, okay? So what's the deal with you and that dog, Chris? Is this some kind of trick?"

Holly was startled when her best friend ran out of the kitchen. She heard Ivy shouting something at Chris—something about the dog.

Holly hurried into the next room. "What's going on, Ives?" she said. "Did Chris do something obnoxious? Because he's like that, you know."

"I was getting the cookies out of the pantry, like you asked." Ivy kept her glare trained on Chris and Peppermint Bark. "I overheard Chris and, you know, him . . ." She nodded at the dog. "They were talking about, like, portals and the North Pole and stuff . . ."

Holly shook her head. "What do you mean, they were *talking*? I know Chris likes to pretend he can understand what that dog is saying, but . . ."

"Not just Chris." Ivy turned to face her. "I can understand him too."

"What?" Chris exclaimed.

The dog started barking excitedly, but Holly ignored him. "Seriously, Ives," she said. "Don't play into his silly games, or we'll never get him to leave us alone."

"I *am* serious." Ivy stared at her. "When he barks, I hear words." She glanced at the dog as he barked again. "For instance, he just said, 'Hooray! You must have true Christmas spirit.'"

"Yeah, right." Holly rolled her eyes, but there was something about the serious look on Ivy's face that made her wonder. Dogs couldn't talk—could they?

She turned to stare at Peppermint Bark. He gazed back happily, his tongue lolling out of his mouth. Then he barked again.

Holly squinted, wondering if she was going crazy. She hadn't heard words, exactly. But there was . . . something . . .

"Peppermint Bark says you have to listen with your heart," Chris told her.

Ivy nodded. "I heard it too." She looked from Peppermint Bark to Chris. "So it's true? He's Santa's puppy?"

Chris nodded, and Peppermint Bark barked again. Holly frowned, feeling a little left out.

"Santa's puppy?" she said. "Are you kidding me with this?"

"No." Her little brother gazed at her earnestly. "He accidentally got left behind by Santa's sleigh. Now he needs our help."

Ivy was still watching Peppermint Bark. "So you live at the North Pole?" she asked tentatively. "And there are portals? I always wondered how Santa could travel around the whole world in one night . . . Wait, but what about the reindeer? Can they really fly? And are there, you know, elves and stuff?"

Holly knew that her friend was fascinated by magic and folklore and things like that. And she wasn't a baby, like Chris. If Ivy said Peppermint Bark was Santa's puppy, well, Holly would have to believe her.

"So hold on," Holly said, interrupting the dog's barking. "The idea is, we have to find some kind of magical portal to get him back to the North Pole?"

"Yes, something like that," Ivy said. "This is amazing! I've always wanted to meet an elf."

"So you'll help us find a portal?" Chris asked his sister and Ivy, his face hopeful. "We'd probably be able to figure it out fast if all of us work together . . ."

Holly hesitated, still not quite daring to believe this was really happening. She looked from her brother to her best friend, her gaze finally settling on the dog. The dog with the eerily intelligent eyes and the barks that almost sounded like words . . .

7

North Pole AWOL

"Hurry, hurry!" Juniper's urgent, high-pitched voice interrupted the rest of the elves, who were singing Christmas carols as they tidied their workshop. "Mrs. Claus will be here soon to inspect the premises. This workshop needs to look as fresh as new-fallen snow!"

Happy quickly swept the sawdust beneath his workbench into a pile. Nearby, an elf named Mistletoe wiped down her bench. She let out a soft snort. "That Juniper is awfully bossy, isn't she?" she whispered to Happy. "Plus she's doing more supervising than cleaning, if you ask me!"

Happy chuckled. "Juniper loves to supervise," he

agreed. "That's why she's been such a super Head Elf this year."

"True, but Mrs. Claus won't be here for hours." Mistletoe shook out her rag. "She always spends Christmas morning cross-country skiing and monitoring the weather for Santa's journey on that solar-powered weather station thingamabob she invented a few years ago. She probably won't even come back to the castle until it's time to take the Christmas cookies out of the oven."

"I know. But we should finish tidying up as fast as we can anyway," Happy reminded Mistletoe. "Mrs. Claus will be here eventually, and she can spot a tool out of place at fifty paces. Besides, Santa will be back as soon as the last time zone on Earth strikes midnight to end Christmas Day. And then we'll need to get back to work making toys for next year."

Happy couldn't wait! Making toys was the only thing he thought about—morning, noon, and night. Well, that and *playing with* toys . . . He had to admit that Juniper, Peppermint Bark, and even Santa himself had caught him doing that a few times over the past year!

Mistletoe was smiling now too. All elves loved making toys. Even Juniper looked almost cheerful when she was doing it.

"Okay, everyone!" an elf on the other side of the room called out. "How about we sing 'Deck the Halls' next? *Deck the halls with boughs of holly . . .*"

"*Fa-la-la-la-la . . .*" Happy sang along with the rest of the elves. Then he glanced over at Juniper. She was the only one not singing. Instead, she was standing at the top of the stone steps leading down into the workshop, her sharp eyes darting around the room to watch what the others were doing.

Suddenly the door behind her flew open. Mrs. Claus stood there, dressed in bright green ski pants, a red knitted cap, and a peppermint-striped parka with a mobile weather monitor poking out of one pocket. But instead of looking happy and excited to explore the tundra, her face was worried.

"Hello, everyone—don't let me disturb you," she said. "But have any of you seen Peppermint Bark lately?"

"Peppermint Bark?" Juniper echoed. "No—come to think of it, he hasn't been helping with the cleanup at all."

"That's true," an elf called out from the far end of

the room. "Usually he loves to chase the stray ribbons and wires into the trash bin."

"And gobble up any leftover peppermints," another elf added.

Happy giggled. "And bark along with our singing, even though he usually gets the words wrong—like, *Deck the halls with bow-wows of holly*..."

Mrs. Claus chuckled, but she also started pacing back and forth. She always had lots of energy—she had to, to keep the snow castle and workshop running smoothly, maintain all the tech and equipment, and still enjoy her favorite snow sports—and rarely stood still for long. But this was different.

"Well, I haven't seen hide nor hair of that hungry pup all day," she said. "He usually goes with me on my Christmas Day ski trek, but there's no sign of him, even though I should have been out on the trails half an hour ago. He didn't even show up to lick the dough bowl when I mixed up the Christmas cookies earlier!"

Happy was surprised to hear that. Peppermint Bark loved Mrs. Claus's special Christmas Day cookie dough just as much as Happy loved making toys!

"I hope he's okay," he said, so concerned that he forgot to feel shy about speaking up in front of everyone. "Maybe we should help you search for him."

"Yes! We'll help!" several other elves chorused.

Juniper frowned. "But we haven't finished tidying up yet."

"That can wait." Mrs. Claus stopped pacing and looked around, her brow furrowed beneath the brim of her ski cap. "We need to find Peppermint Bark first. What if something's happened to him?"

Happy shuddered at the thought. But he tried to stay positive. "I'm sure it will only take a short time to find Peppermint Bark with all of us helping," he said.

Mistletoe nodded. "We'll go back to tidying as soon as we find him."

"Hooray!" most of the other elves cheered.

Juniper shrugged and sighed. "All right, let's look for that silly pup," she said. "As long as you all promise we'll get back to work as soon as we find him!"

But they didn't find him. Happy and the others searched every nook and cranny of the snow castle. They checked upstairs and downstairs and in both towers. They checked the basement, where the furnace clanked and flared, and the shed, where Santa kept his sleigh out of the snow. They checked the kitchen and the closets and inside the big clawfoot bathtub. A couple of elves even went out to search the stable where the reindeer lived.

There was no sign of Peppermint Bark in any of those places. Finally, everyone gathered in the workshop once again. The elves had kept singing the whole time they searched. But nobody was singing now.

"Oh dear," Mrs. Claus said, pacing more frantically than ever. "What could have become of Peppermint Bark?"

Happy had been thinking about that exact question. And he'd come up with an answer. He raised his hand. "I have an idea," he said shyly. "Er, more of a theory, really . . ."

All eyes turned to him. "You're good friends with Peppermint Bark, aren't you?" Mistletoe said. "What is it, Happy? Where do you think he could be?"

Happy took a deep breath. "I wonder . . . I wonder if he might have . . ." He gulped, hoping he wasn't getting his friend in big trouble. "Um, that is, what if he stowed away on Santa's sleigh?"

A gasp went up from the elves. "Stowed away?" Juniper exclaimed. "Impossible! Santa told him he wasn't allowed to go."

Some of the other elves nodded. A few echoed Juniper's "Impossible!"

But Mrs. Claus stopped pacing and looked thoughtful. "Stowed away, eh?" she said. "Do you really think he might have done that, Happy?"

Happy shrugged. "He wanted to ride along to help Santa on his rounds," he said. "He wanted it more than anything!"

"It's the only theory that makes sense, then," Mrs. Claus said.

Happy smiled, feeling proud of himself for thinking of it. Then his smile faded as he realized what it meant if he was right. Peppermint Bark could be in big trouble!

Mrs. Claus looked more worried than ever. "There's a reason Santa didn't want that pup riding along," she reminded the elves. "He's so young and happy-go-lucky and full of energy, he won't want to sit in the sleigh the whole time. And as focused as Santa gets on Christmas, well, I'm afraid he might not notice if Peppermint Bark were to hop out and wander off . . ."

"Oh no!" an elf exclaimed. "What will become of Peppermint Bark if he gets left behind?"

"Nothing good, that's for sure," Juniper said. "Santa

doesn't have time to stop and search for him. And I doubt that silly pup would be able to find a portal back here on his own — does he even know how the portals work?"

Happy shrugged. "I don't know," he admitted. "I'm not sure I understand how they work either."

"Oh dear." Mrs. Claus looked around at the elves. "We have to do something! Someone needs to go out there and find Peppermint Bark before Christmas Day ends." She sighed and touched the weather equipment sticking out of her pocket. "I wish I could go myself, but I need to monitor the satellites and notify Santa if he has to change course . . ."

Most of the elves looked confused, nervous, or both. But Juniper stepped forward with a determined tilt to her jaw.

"I'll do it," she volunteered. "I'm Head Elf; it should be me who goes."

Happy couldn't help being impressed. Juniper might be a little bossy, but she sure was brave! He couldn't imagine how scary it must be out there in the rest of the world, far from their safe, snug home here at the North Pole . . .

"Thank you, Juniper," Mrs. Claus said. "But you

can't go alone." She scanned the gathered elves, then pointed. "Happy, you probably know Peppermint Bark better than anyone. Would you go with Juniper?"

Happy gulped. "M-me?"

"Him?" Juniper shot Happy a dubious look. "That's not necessary, Mrs. C, really. I can handle it on my own."

"No—it will be risky enough going out into the world." Mrs. Claus looked very serious. "You won't have much time to find Peppermint Bark and get back here before the gates close."

Happy closed his eyes for a moment. That did sound risky! But then he thought about how scared Peppermint Bark must be right now.

He opened his eyes, took a deep breath, and nodded. "I'll do it," he said. "I want to help Peppermint Bark."

"Fine." Juniper squared her shoulders. "But you'd better be prepared to keep up. Because like Mrs. C said, we won't have much time."

All the elves came along as Happy and Juniper went outside with Mrs. Claus. "Please stay on your toes, you two," she told them as they all tromped through the snow toward the peppermint-striped gates. "Humans aren't used to seeing elves in their world. You'll have to be very, very careful not to let them figure out who—and what—you really are. It will help that it's Christmas, and everyone should be in a happy holiday mood. But still . . ." Her voice trailed off, and her bright blue eyes were anxious.

"Don't worry about me, Mrs. C," Juniper said. She glanced at Happy. "Uh, I mean, don't worry about us. We'll find Peppermint Bark and be home in time to enjoy those cookies you're baking."

Happy breathed in the warm, familiar scent of half-baked cookies drifting from the snow castle on the chilly breeze. Would he really get to taste those cookies?

A wise old elf named Tannenbaum started explaining how the portal system worked. Happy was too nervous to take in much of it. All he heard was that the portals could take the elves anywhere on Earth—and that the best way to find them was to search for the scent of pinecones and gingerbread.

"Got it," Juniper said when Tannenbaum finished. "Now let's get moving. We're burning Christmas Daylight."

By then all the elves had reached the gates, which stood wide open as they always did on Christmas Day. Happy looked up at the grand entrance. He'd never been outside those gates before. Before he could wonder what awaited him Out There, Juniper yanked him through.

"Good luck!" Mrs. Claus called, already sounding very far away. The rest of the elves were singing again, but Happy could hardly hear them over the nervous pounding of his heart.

Inside the gates, everything was a winter wonderland. Out here it was winter too, but with none of the twinkling, homey Christmas cheer. The landscape was barren and windswept, with only a few gnarled trees visible through the blowing snow. Somewhere far in the distance there rose an eerie howl.

"W-w-where's the portal?" Happy asked through teeth chattering with cold and fear.

Juniper looked around. "I think that's it."

She pointed at something that looked like a mini whirlwind twirling wildly just above the icy ground. Happy stared at it, mesmerized—and gasped when Juniper grabbed him by the arm and leaped right into it.

"Waaaaaah!" he cried as he felt himself spinning around and around and around . . .

8

There Goes Santa Claus

Chris could hardly believe it. His sister actually seemed to accept that Peppermint Bark was Santa's puppy! And to think Chris had been starting to wonder if she had any Christmas spirit left!

This is great, he thought. *Maybe there's still a little bit of the old Holly in there after all . . .*

"So we should start searching right away," he urged, kicking aside a crumpled piece of wrapping paper on the living room floor. "We don't have much time."

"Yes, please!" Peppermint Bark danced around Holly's feet. "I have to get back before the gates close."

"The gates?" Chris glanced down at him.

Peppermint Bark nodded. "Big, beautiful gates that separate the North Pole from the rest of the world," he explained. "They stay shut all year except for Christmas Day. When the last time zone on Earth strikes midnight tonight, they'll shut again—and not even Santa can open them until next Christmas." The little dog shivered. "If I'm not back by then, I'm stuck here for a whole year."

For a second, Chris's heart leaped with hope. If Peppermint Bark got stuck here, maybe Chris could figure out a way for them to stay together . . .

Ivy was telling Holly what the little dog had just said. "He might be stuck somewhere," Holly commented, glancing at Peppermint Bark. "But it won't be here. Not with Dad's allergies."

Chris's heart sank. His sister was right. Besides, he didn't want to force his new friend to stay if he was homesick. Peppermint Bark wanted to get home to the North Pole, and that meant Chris wanted to help him. No matter how much it hurt to think of the little dog going away . . .

"Like I said, we don't have much time," Chris said quickly, before he could think too much about that. He spun and headed toward the front door. "So let's get out there and start searching for portals!"

"Yes, let's go!" Peppermint Bark exclaimed.

Holly held up a hand. "No way—you're not leaving this house," she told her brother. "Mom said so. You stay here, and Ivy and I will look for this portal thingy."

Chris's jaw dropped. "What? No!" he retorted. "Mom told you to stay inside too."

"But this is an emergency!" Ivy exclaimed. "We're looking for elves—I mean, portals!"

"Right. And we'll be able to move faster without you," Holly said, not quite meeting Chris's eye. "Right, Ives?"

Chris scowled, expecting Ivy to back up her friend —like always. But she bit her lip and didn't say anything.

"No!" Peppermint Bark barked. "We should all go together!"

Ivy shrugged. "The dog wants us to stick together," she told Holly. "Anyway, your parents might be mad if we leave Chris here by himself, since he's so young and stuff."

Chris wanted to protest—he might be young, but

he was obviously more mature than the two girls! But Holly was nodding, so he didn't say that.

Instead he sat on the edge of the couch to get closer to Peppermint Bark. "So these portals—how will we know where to find one?" he asked.

"I'm not sure." The little dog stared up at him, looking uncertain. "All I know is that they smell like gingerbread and pinecones, just like the North Pole. And they're disguised so humans won't see them."

"So we have to go around smelling everything in town?" Ivy wrinkled her nose. "That doesn't sound very efficient."

"Huh? What?" Holly glanced from her brother to her best friend, looking annoyed. "Wait, what'd he say? I think I heard him say something about smell, but that's all I got . . ."

Chris wondered if Holly was telling the truth. Was she starting to understand Peppermint Bark? Or was she just trying to fit in by pretending she did, latching on to the word she'd heard Ivy say? That sort of seemed like something his sister might do, especially lately.

Ivy was already telling Holly what the dog had said. "So I'm not sure how we're supposed to find one of these portals," Ivy said with a little frown. "Anyway, it doesn't make sense. In fairy tales and stuff, there's always a special way to locate something. You know, like a trail of bread crumbs or a magic spell or something."

"This isn't a fairy tale, it's real life," Chris reminded her.

Ivy was staring at the Christmas tree twinkling and gleaming nearby. "The portals smell like Christmas stuff, right?" she said slowly. "So people can't see them, but they can *smell* them . . ."

"We've covered this already." Holly sounded impatient. "Maybe we should just go out and start smelling around."

"No, wait." Peppermint Bark stepped closer to Ivy. "What are you thinking?"

Ivy glanced down at the dog. "Be careful, you're getting too close to the tree," she told him. "Your tail might knock off some ornaments." She scooted around him and moved away. "Anyway, I was just thinking it would be weird to smell gingerbread and pinecones in, like, the bus station or on some random street corner. But it would seem normal at the holiday market. Or the town square where the big Christmas tree is."

Chris gasped. "That makes sense. We need to look in Christmasy places!"

"Yes, yes!" Peppermint Bark spun in an excited circle. His wagging tail hit a couple of ornaments on the tree, but not even Ivy said anything about that. The kids were all talking at once, listing off all the Christmasy places in town.

There was just one problem. This was Poinsettia, which meant there were a *lot* of Christmasy places.

"We have to start somewhere," Chris said. "So which spot seems most likely?"

His sister shrugged. "You mean if I were Santa, where would I put a portal?" she said. "Probably in a place connected with me." She clapped her hands. "I know! The post office! Kids send their letters to Santa through there, right? And there's a huge Christmas wreath in the lobby—I saw it when Dad and I stopped by to mail our gifts to Grandma last week."

Ivy gasped. "Maybe the wreath is the portal! All the portals I've seen in movies and stuff were round like a wreath, anyway."

Chris wasn't sure the post office was the most Christmasy place in Poinsettia. But as he said, they had to start somewhere. "Let's check it out," he said, heading toward the front door with Peppermint Bark on his heels. He brushed past Ivy, who jumped aside and looked at the dog.

"Hold on," Ivy said. "You can't just let that dog run around town loose. We need a leash."

"No we don't," Chris said. "Peppermint Bark isn't an ordinary dog, remember? He's not going to run off or chase the neighbor's cat or anything. Right, buddy?"

"Sure!" Peppermint Bark said. "What's a cat?"

"No, Ivy's right," Holly said. "There's a leash law in this town. If anyone sees him running free, we'll get in trouble."

"What's a leash?" Peppermint Bark asked Chris.

Chris sighed. He thought the girls were being silly, but there was no time to argue. Besides, maybe they were right. If some busybody like Mr. Brooks or nosy old Mrs. O'Toole down the block spotted Peppermint Bark running loose, it could delay their quest.

Chris quickly explained what a collar and leash were to the little dog. Peppermint Bark looked confused, but he nodded.

"Okay, let's get me a collar and leash," he said cheerfully.

"Wait—where are we going to get that stuff?" Holly asked. "Maybe we can ask the Garcias to borrow one."

"Their dog's collar would be too big for Peppermint Bark. Anyway, I have a better idea." Chris grabbed the box with the Christmas tie he'd given his dad. "This should work," he said, pulling out the tie. "As for a leash, hmm . . . wait here!"

He dashed upstairs. Seconds later he was rummaging through his parents' closet. Aha! There it was . . .

Back downstairs, he showed Peppermint Bark his new leash — also known as Dad's Santa-print belt. "Perfect!" Peppermint Bark said as Chris threaded the tie through the belt buckle and knotted it loosely around Peppermint Bark's furry white neck.

"Good," Ivy said, watching carefully. "You should hold on to him the whole time we're out there, okay?"

"Whatever." Chris wasn't sure why she was so stuck on the leash thing, and like so many things about Ivy, he really didn't care. "Let's go."

They trooped out to the front closet and put on their coats and gloves. Ivy wrapped her new ivy-embroidered scarf around her neck. Then she opened the front door.

Peppermint Bark was right behind her. When he looked out, he pricked up his ears. "Oh, wow!" he barked loudly, pushing past Ivy. "I can't believe this!"

"Hey!" Ivy jumped back, bumping into Chris.

"Watch it!" Chris had been pulling on his gloves. The makeshift leash slipped out of his hand. "Whoa, Peppermint Bark, wait for us!"

But it was too late—the little dog raced out the door.

"It's Santa!" Peppermint Bark cried happily, his tail wagging so fast it was a blur. "Hey, guys, he's here!"

"Santa!" Peppermint Bark's heart pounded as he hurtled across the front yard. That leash thingy the kids had attached to him was trailing behind, making a funny flapping sound in the wind, but he hardly noticed. "Santa, I'm here! Wait for me-e-e-e-e-e!"

The puppy had spotted the jolly old man immediately. He was up on a rooftop across the street waving at Peppermint Bark. The sleigh was right beside him, looking a little precarious balanced above the front porch.

"I knew you'd come back for me!" Peppermint Bark barked happily as he raced across the street.

Behind him came the faint sound of Chris and the others shouting. But Peppermint Bark was completely focused on reaching Santa before the reindeer took off again.

"I'm coming!" he cried, flinging himself onto a shrub covered in twinkling multicolored lights. The woven net of cords tangled around his leash and caught on one hind paw, but that hardly slowed him down. He leaped upward, dragging the lights with him, scrabbling wildly at the edge of the porch railing. Then it was one more leap into a huge hanging basket of holly and pine boughs draped with ribbons.

"Whoa!" Peppermint Bark cried as the basket creaked and swung under his weight. "Yikes!"

He scrambled upward, his front claws barely grabbing the rain gutter as the basket came loose and crashed to the ground. Oops! Well, he was sure Santa could fix that . . .

"Santa!" he cried, pulling himself up onto the porch roof. But the string of lights was still dangling from his hind foot and seemed to be stuck on something. Drat!

There was a thick green cord snaking across the roof right in front of him. Peppermint Bark grabbed it in his teeth to anchor himself. Then he gave one more kick to loosen the lights from his hind foot . . . and this time felt something give way.

"Look out!" Chris cried from somewhere below. "Peppermint Bark, you're going to pull over the . . . Oops."

Peppermint Bark glanced over his shoulder, which pulled the thick green cord in his teeth farther down toward the edge of the roof. Below, he saw that the twinkling lights had been attached to a decorative lamppost, which had just tipped over—in turn bringing down more strings of lights and several large balloons.

"Look out!" Holly pointed at something behind Peppermint Bark.

There was an ominous creaking sound. "Uh-oh," Peppermint Bark murmured, turning back to look at the roof.

CRE-E-E-E-EAK!

It was the sleigh! Pulling on the cord had yanked it loose! The sleigh slid slowly, scraping over the shingles, tilting sideways . . .

"Santa, be careful!" Peppermint Bark cried as he saw his friend tipping toward the edge of the roof.

Then Peppermint Bark blinked. Wait—now that he was closer, there was something odd about Santa . . .

"Peppermint Bark, get out of the way!" Chris cried from below. "The whole thing's coming down!"

"Santa?" Peppermint Bark whimpered.

But it *wasn't* Santa—not the real one, anyway. Peppermint Bark could see that now. The plastic smile. The overly red dots on the round cheeks and bulbous nose. The enormous belly, much larger than the real Santa's now that Mrs. Claus had convinced him to go hiking with her more often. Not to mention the reindeer—there were only four of them rather than eight, and while one of them looked a little like Prancer, the others . . .

"Peppermint Bark! Move!" Chris screamed, breaking into the little dog's thoughts.

Peppermint Bark's eyes widened as he saw that the sleigh was skidding straight toward him, coming faster and faster . . .

"Aaaaah!" he cried, his paws losing their grip on the roof. "Oof!"

He landed in the basket of greens that had fallen before. The pointy holly branches poked him painfully, but he couldn't worry about that. He grabbed the edge of the basket with his teeth and flipped it over on top of himself, huddling beneath the protective dome as the holiday display came crashing down . . .

Chris held his breath as the huge sleigh, reindeer, and Santa Claus came crashing down from the Oumas' roof. As soon as the chaos was over, he raced forward. "Peppermint Bark?" he cried. "Where are you?"

"He's got to be okay." Holly sounded worried. "Come on, help me move this stuff!"

But before Chris could panic, a familiar furry white head popped into view. Peppermint Bark was on the porch, crawling out from beneath the hanging basket he'd knocked down. The plastic sleigh and other stuff had missed him and landed farther out on the lawn. Whew!

But Chris's relief didn't last long. The front door opened, revealing a surprised-looking middle-aged couple.

Chris gulped, then smiled weakly. "Hi, Mr. and Mrs. Ouma. Uh, merry Christmas?"

9

Good Tidyings for Christmas

Chris could tell that the Oumas weren't happy about having their holiday display ruined. Mr. Ouma had a funny little crease in his forehead that wasn't usually there. And Mrs. Ouma kept wringing her hands and saying, "Oh my goodness."

"We're really sorry," Chris told them, grabbing the end of Peppermint Bark's makeshift leash. "Um, we just rescued this dog, and—"

Mrs. Ouma brightened immediately. "Oh, he's a rescue?" She leaned down for a closer look at the little dog. "How nice! That explains why he isn't very well trained yet, I suppose."

Chris traded a look with the two girls. "Um, yeah," Holly said. "Anyway, he pulled away when Chris was supposed to be holding on to him . . ."—she paused just long enough to shoot her brother a dirty look— "and I guess he was, like, trying to chase the reindeer or something?"

Ivy giggled nervously. "Yeah, he might have thought they were real," she offered. "They look really great." She glanced at the fake reindeer, now lying jumbled together on the lawn. "Um, they did, anyway . . ."

"Thanks." Mr. Ouma sighed and rubbed his face as he looked around. "We were hoping . . . well, never mind."

"Anyway, he jumped and climbed his way up onto the roof and I guess his paw caught on a cord or something?" Holly shrugged. "And then . . . *kaboom.*"

"We can help you clean up the mess," Ivy offered.

Holly nodded. "Yeah, we feel really bad about it."

"Don't feel bad—it was an accident," Mrs. Ouma assured them, finally dredging up what looked like a real smile. "I know you're good kids. How could you know your new rescue dog was such a talented climber?"

Mr. Ouma was still staring at the mess. "Yes, I'm

sure I can put things back together before the contest judging," he said. He checked his watch. "Probably . . ."

Chris let out a silent sigh of relief. He felt bad about the mess too. But they didn't have much time to get Peppermint Bark home. That was much more important than some silly holiday decorating contest, right?

But Ivy stepped forward. "No, we insist," she said in her polite talking-to-adults voice. "It will be easier with all of us helping. Besides, it was our dog that messed it up."

Chris stiffened. Beside him, he barely heard Holly whisper, "Ives! They said it was okay!"

But Mrs. Ouma was already nodding and smiling. "Thank you, dear," she said. "Maybe that would be best."

"Yes." Mr. Ouma sounded relieved. "It took three people to get that sleigh up there. I'm not sure I could even do it by myself. Just give me a second to grab my coat and gloves and we can get started."

He and his wife hurried back inside. Chris spun to glare at Ivy.

"Are you crazy?" he exclaimed. "This is going to take forever!"

"Yeah," Holly added. "They already said we didn't have to help, Ives!"

Ivy shrugged, looking stubborn. "It's the right thing to do," she insisted.

Chris sighed loudly. But Peppermint Bark nudged his leg. "Ivy is right," the little dog barked. "We—I mean, I—caused this mess. It's only right that we should help fix it."

Ivy smiled slightly. "Exactly."

"But we don't have much time until—" Chris began.

His sister elbowed him sharply. The Oumas had just returned. "Okay, kids," Mr. Ouma said cheerfully, clapping his gloved hands briskly. "Ready to get to work?"

Peppermint Bark wished he could do more to help. But every time he got anywhere near the decorations, the adults looked suspicious. Finally he just sat back and watched as the kids and the Oumas worked.

It took a little more than an hour before everything was more or less back the way it had been. Now that he was thinking clearly, Peppermint Bark could hardly believe he'd mistaken the plastic Santa for the real thing. The fake one was not only a little fatter, his nose was bigger and his beard was shorter. Not to mention that the reindeer were too small, too few, and not even the right color . . .

Finally the Oumas seemed satisfied. "I'm not sure it's a prize-winning display, but it'll do," Mr. Ouma said, plugging in the last set of lights. "Thanks for helping put it back together, kids."

His wife nodded. "It's awfully chilly out here," she said with a dramatic shiver. "Won't you all come in for some hot cocoa?"

"Oh, thank you!" Ivy said.

"Thanks, but we've really got to go," Chris said at the same time, shooting Ivy a glare.

Ivy cleared her throat. "Um, Chris is right. We should go," she said politely. "But thanks for the offer! Merry Christmas!"

Peppermint Bark trotted along at Chris's heels as the kids waved goodbye to the Oumas and hurried down the sidewalk. "Sorry about that, you guys," he barked.

"It's okay—you didn't mean to," Chris said. "But from now on, check with me before you run off, okay?"

"Sure, Chris." Peppermint Bark wagged his tail.

Chris glanced at the girls. "Now we really have to hurry," he said. "Let's get to the post office as fast as we can, okay? Because we have even less time than we did before, thanks to a certain someone."

For a second Peppermint Bark thought Chris was talking about him. But then Ivy frowned. "I told you, it was the right thing to do!" she snapped.

Chris rolled his eyes and glanced at his sister. Holly shrugged. "Yeah, Ives is right," she said. "We had to help fix that mess."

"What?" Chris sounded wounded, though Peppermint Bark wasn't sure exactly why. "Okay, whatever. The post office is this way." Chris sped up, walking so fast that Peppermint Bark had to break into a trot to keep up.

The girls followed. "Hey, wait, I just thought of something," Holly said as they neared the end of the block. "It's Christmas Day. Isn't everything closed today?"

"Not Jingle Junction — that's open all day," Ivy said. "I think the supermarket might be open too, at least for part of the day, and the International Center at PVU, and maybe also —"

"Okay, not my point, Ives," Holly interrupted. "What about the post office?"

"Oh." Chris's face fell. "Actually, I think you're right. It's closed today. We won't be able to get inside to check out that wreath."

Peppermint Bark was about to ask what they meant. But they'd just rounded the corner . . . and he caught a whiff of a familiar scent.

"Gingerbread and pinecones!" he barked excitedly. "It's a portal!"

10

Postmark: Christmas

"Stop!" Chris cried as the little dog yanked the leash out of his hand and took off. "Peppermint Bark, you promised not to do that!"

"But I'm sure this time!" Peppermint Bark cried. "It's a portal—I can see it now! It's at the bottom of that big Christmas tree!"

Chris looked ahead. Half a block away was the little municipal complex consisting of the town hall, the post office, and a couple of other official buildings. In the middle of them was an enormous Christmas tree. Was there really a portal there? It made sense . . .

"Wait!" Chris called, breaking into a run. Was Peppermint Bark going to leave without even saying good-bye? "I just want to . . ."

"Christopher Kerstman!" a stern voice rang out nearby. "Stop where you are, young man!"

Chris skidded to a stop. Nobody in town dared to disobey that voice. He turned to see a white-haired man with a tidy mustache and very upright posture striding toward him. "Um, hi, Mr. Brooks," Chris said. "Merry Christmas."

"And a very merry Christmas to you, too." Mr. Brooks nodded sharply and straightened his red-and-green-plaid bow tie. "Is that your dog?"

By then Holly and Ivy had caught up. "Hi, Mr. Brooks," Holly said breathlessly. "Sorry about that. We had him on a leash, but he got away."

"There are laws about loose dogs in this town, you know." The old man glanced toward Peppermint Bark, who was racing toward the tree.

Chris looked that way too, and his heart sank. Peppermint Bark was almost there. And now, if Chris squinted slightly, he was pretty sure he could see a funny swirling shape in the tree's lower branches, like a whirlpool in the air.

The portal, he thought. *I guess I won't get to say good-bye after all . . .*

"I'm coming, Santa!" Peppermint Bark barked as he hurled himself toward the Christmas tree. "I'm coming!"

The portal swirled and swirled, just like the one he'd seen through the gates at the North Pole. The delicious, homey scents of gingerbread and pinecones washed out toward him, pulling him forward.

Wow, that was easier than I thought, Peppermint Bark told himself happily. *I'm going home! All thanks to Chris and his friends . . .*

The little dog stopped in front of the portal and turned to thank the kids for everything they'd done. To his surprise, they were still half a block back. A stern-looking older man was shaking a finger at them. Then the man turned and pointed—straight at Peppermint Bark!

"Uh-oh," Peppermint Bark said. "Did I get them in trouble again?"

He glanced at the portal. Was it his imagination, or did it look a little smaller than it had a moment ago? No, it wasn't his imagination—even as he watched, it shrank a little more. Peppermint Bark wasn't sure what that meant, but he could guess.

It's closing! he thought with a gulp. *I might not have much time . . .*

Then he looked at the kids down the block. He couldn't let them get in trouble—again—because of him. Besides, the portal wasn't that small yet. He still had time . . .

Peppermint Bark raced back to the kids. The man was saying something about leash laws and community standards and town supervisor meetings. Peppermint Bark didn't understand much of it, but he could guess what had started the lecture.

"Pick up my leash," he barked softly at Chris. "Maybe that will help."

Chris nodded and grabbed the belt, which had been dragging behind Peppermint Bark. "See? He's on the leash again," Chris told the man.

"Harrumph." The man looked down his beaklike nose at Peppermint Bark. "Even so, it's important for you youngsters to realize . . ."

"Nice try," Holly muttered to Chris, just loudly enough for Peppermint Bark to hear. "You know you can't stop Mr. Brooks once he gets his scold on."

Peppermint Bark stared up at the man, who looked grumpy—far too grumpy for anyone to be on Christmas!

Peppermint Bark wagged his tail, letting out a soft chime of jingle bells. Peppermint Bark could tell that Chris heard it—and Ivy, too. Even Holly glanced at him in surprise.

Mr. Brooks didn't look down at Peppermint Bark, but his expression softened slightly as the puppy's Christmas magic washed over him. "Well, never mind," he said in a gruff but friendlier tone. "It's Christmas, eh? Just try not to let it happen again, all right?"

"We won't," Holly assured him.

Just then there was a tinkle of melody from somewhere on the man. Peppermint Bark pricked up his ears, recognizing the tune—"The Twelve Days of Christmas," one of the elves' favorites to sing while they worked.

Mr. Brooks pulled a cell phone from his pocket and glanced at it. "I'd better go," he told the kids, tucking the phone away again. "They need me at the festival setup." He hurried off, still muttering under his breath. "I do declare, if I don't attend to every last detail myself, something is sure to go wrong . . ."

As soon as the man disappeared around the corner, Peppermint Bark whirled to face the kids. "You were right, Holly!" he barked. "There's a portal at the post office—but it's outside in the tree, not inside in the wreath!"

"He says you were right, Hols," Ivy translated. "There's one of the portals outside—"

"In the tree," Holly finished for her, looking a bit stunned. "Yeah, I think . . . I think I got that part."

Chris looked surprised. "You understood him?"

Peppermint Bark was glad that Holly seemed to be getting her Christmas spirit back. But he didn't have time to congratulate her. "We have to hurry!" he urged the kids. "The portals—they don't all stay open the whole time. When Santa is finished with one, it might close early. And this one looks like it's closing!"

Chris gasped. "Let's go!"

They ran toward the Christmas tree. Peppermint Bark was leading the way. But when they got closer, the little dog could see that the portal was smaller now—much smaller.

"I have to go!" he cried. "I'm sorry there's not much time for goodbyes. Thank you for helping me, and merry Christmas!"

He glanced at the kids, especially Chris, knowing he would miss this new friend most of all. Chris smiled at him. Then the boy glanced at the tree and gasped.

"Hurry!" he cried. "You have to go now!"

Peppermint Bark spun around, leaped forward . . . and crashed into the prickly branches of the tree.

"Oh no!" Ivy exclaimed behind him. "You're too late. The portal is gone!"

11

A Happy Holiday

"Oof! Portals are crazy!" Happy exclaimed as he and Juniper tumbled out onto the ground. He sat up and held his head in both hands. "Whoa! When will everything stop spinning?"

Juniper jumped to her feet. "Shake it off, elf," she ordered. "We have work to do."

Happy climbed to his feet, still dizzy. Traveling through the portal had been like being inside a sparkly, spinning Christmas ornament. The sounds of cheery Christmas carols had surrounded them, and the scents of pinecones and gingerbread were even stronger than

they were at the North Pole. It was fun, but a little be-
fuddling.

Happy blinked a few times to clear his mind, then
looked around. Wherever they'd landed looked quite a
bit like the North Pole. There was a thin dusting of snow
on the ground. Everywhere he looked, he saw candy
canes, tinsel, and pine boughs. There were even a few
reindeer standing in the distance, though they looked a
bit stiff. And there, surrounded by excited children, was
a jolly red-suited fellow with a white beard who looked
an awful lot like . . .

"Santa!" Happy blurted out. "Hey, Juniper, look!
Santa's here! Now we can tell him about Peppermint
Bark, and find out if he's still in the sleigh, and . . ."

He started to dash toward the red-suited man. But
Juniper grabbed him by the ear, yanking him back.

"Stop!" she said. "That's not Santa, silly."

Happy blinked and rubbed his ear, looking from Juniper to the red-suited man and back again. "It's not?"

"No." Juniper shook her head so hard that her long
nose waggled back and forth. "Take a closer look. It's
not Santa—just someone dressed like him. It must be
one of those human helpers he's told us about."

"Human helpers?" That sounded familiar, though Happy couldn't quite remember what Santa had said.

Juniper nodded. "Humans who dress up like Santa," she explained. "They find out what children want for Christmas and spread holiday cheer." She glanced toward the helper, who had just lifted a tiny tot onto his lap. "The smaller children actually believe whichever helper is there is the real Santa. But of course, the older ones know better."

"Wow." Happy was a little disappointed. "So that's not Santa."

"Of course not. Anyway, use your noggin." Juniper tapped the brim of her hat. "It's daytime here, which means the real Santa has already come and gone. He likes to make sure the children's gifts are waiting under the tree first thing Christmas morning."

"Oh, okay." Happy glanced over his shoulder at the portal, which was located in a wall of fake snow behind where the Santa helper was sitting. "Then why did the portal spit us out here? It's magical, after all—I thought it might be sending us straight to Santa."

"Hmm." Juniper rubbed her chin. "That's true, there must be a reason we're here." She snapped her fingers. "I know! Maybe Peppermint Bark is nearby."

Happy clapped his hands. "That must be it!" He looked around. "But where's here?"

Both elves wandered a little farther from the portal. As soon as they came out from behind the mass of excited children, Happy could see that they were in some sort of outdoor holiday market. There were stands selling hand-knit Christmas stockings, hot apple cider, snowman-shaped balloons, and other festive items. The red-suited Santa helper sat beneath a sign reading **SANTA STATION**. And up ahead, hanging over the whole area, was a sign made of blinking Christmas lights that spelled out **JINGLE JUNCTION**.

"This is probably the most Christmasy spot in this town," Juniper said. "That's why the portal is here. But Peppermint Bark might be anywhere in town."

Happy nodded. "We have to find him!"

"Yes." Juniper's long nose twitched as she smelled the air. "Time to sniff him out and drag him home."

Holly Jolly Christmas

"Back to square one," Chris said with a sigh, staring at the spot where the portal had been. It didn't look any different from the rest of the Christmas tree now. Peppermint Bark had pushed his way in between the branches just to make sure the portal wasn't there somewhere, but he'd finally admitted it was gone.

Holly shrugged. "At least now we know what we're looking for," she pointed out. "I mean, Peppermint Bark is still the only one who can smell the portal from far away. But I could see it pretty well just before it closed."

"Me too," Ivy said. "It was a sort of swirly, shimmering spot in the air—like glimmering snow falling in just that one spot." She wrapped her arms around herself and shivered dramatically. "I can't believe we just saw a portal leading to the North Pole!"

Chris glanced at Peppermint Bark, who looked dejected as he stared up at the Christmas tree. "Is there any chance it might open again?" Chris asked. "We could wait here and see."

"I don't think so," the little dog barked. "Once a portal closes, that's probably it. At least until next Christmas. And I don't want to wait that long to go home."

Chris didn't answer. He still wished Peppermint Bark could stay longer. The more time they spent together, the more Chris wished they could stay together. Was this what it was like to have a best friend—one you wanted to be around all the time? He glanced at his sister and Ivy, wondering if that was how they felt about each other.

Nah, probably not, he told himself. *They just both like doing goofy stuff like shopping for hair barrettes and wearing the same silly necklace . . .*

"Okay, then we should move on," Holly said, turning away from the post office. "Where do we look next? I mean, there have to be lots of portals in a Christmasy place like Poinsettia, right?"

Peppermint Bark brightened. "Right!" he agreed.

Ivy shivered and tucked her hands into the pockets of her coat and her chin into her ivy scarf. "Let's walk while we figure it out," she suggested. "I'm getting cold just standing here."

For the next few minutes, Holly didn't say much. She barely heard her brother and Ivy arguing about where else to look for portals.

That was because she was trying to hide how freaked out she felt. Was this really happening? Was she actually helping a talking dog get home to the North Pole —and his owner, Santa Claus?

Holly thought of herself as a practical person. A realist. Too smart to fall for dumb fantasy stuff like talking animals.

But I saw that portal myself, she thought. *At least, I saw* something—*and if Ivy says it's a portal, I guess I believe her. I mean, I always knew Christmas was kind of magical, and it sort of makes sense that Santa would need a way to get around the world so fast . . .*

Just then a loud snort from Chris brought Holly's

focus back to the conversation. The three kids and Peppermint Bark were almost at the center of town by then, just half a block from Poinsettia Square. Ivy had stopped in front of the display window at Jakobson's Toy Store.

"We don't need to hear all about Christmas folklore around the world, okay?" Chris said to Ivy with a frown.

"But it's really interesting!" Ivy insisted. "Especially the Christmas trolls in Iceland." She waved a hand at the shop window, which featured a few fuzzy-bearded felt trolls among the snowmen and reindeer and penguins in Santa hats. "See, there are thirteen of them, and they come down from the mountains at Christmas to see which boys and girls have been naughty or nice —just like Santa. Kids leave out their shoes, and the trolls leave candy and gifts for the good ones and rotten potatoes for—"

"Just stop!" Chris interrupted. "We're supposed to be helping Peppermint Bark, not studying for a test on Santa Claus! Especially since we're already running out of time, thanks to a certain someone who insisted on helping the Oumas even though they said we didn't have to."

"Leave her alone," Holly told her brother sharply.

"And if you're in such a hurry, come up with a plan, already."

"We don't have time to stop and figure out a plan," Chris said. "That's my point! We have to find another portal!"

"That's what I'm trying to do," Ivy insisted. "I figured since Santa is part of Christmas folklore, and the portals are in Christmasy spots, then thinking about other holiday folklore and stuff might give us a hint where to look."

"I hear you, Ives." Even though she loved her best friend, Holly had to admit that Ivy got lost in her own head sometimes. "But it makes more sense to . . ." Holly trailed off and blinked at something in the little garden between the toy shop and the house next door. "Hey, did you guys see that?"

"See what?" Chris was still glaring at Ivy.

"That." Holly took a step off to the side, peering into a green hedge covered with white twinkling holiday lights. "It looked like . . ." Her words trailed off again. She didn't want to say what she thought she'd just seen.

Now both her brother and her best friend were looking at her. "What?" Ivy asked. "What'd you see, Hols? A portal?"

"No." Holly shook her head. "Not a portal. I thought I saw . . ." She paused and cleared her throat, not quite daring to meet their eyes. "Um, it looked sort of like an . . . an elf."

"Really?" Ivy cried, looking excited.

"No, not really," Holly said quickly. "I mean, it looked like a little person in a long cap sneaking into the shrubbery there. But it was probably just a squirrel or something."

Chris looked dubious. "A squirrel doesn't look much like an elf in a long cap."

"I know. I just think this talking dog thing must be going to my head or something." Holly glanced at Peppermint Bark, whose ears were perked toward the spot she'd pointed out.

"Are you sure that's it?" he barked. "What did you see, exactly?"

Holly shrugged. "Like I said, a little person, maybe yay high"—she held her hand at waist level—"dressed in a long striped cap and—"

"Hols!" Ivy sounded more excited than ever. "Do you realize what just happened?"

"Yeah, I started hallucinating Christmas creatures in the bushes—that's what I was saying," Holly said, rolling her eyes. "Trust me, I know how crazy it sounds, okay?"

Then Chris gasped. "No, I get it," he said. "Holly—you answered Peppermint Bark's question just now. That means you understood what he said! Like, not just a word here or there, but all of it!"

Holly blinked. She looked down at the white puppy, who was gazing up at her with his tongue lolling out and his fuzzy tail wagging rapidly.

"They're right, you know," he barked happily. "You got your Christmas spirit back!"

"I did?" Holly started to smile as she realized he was right. "Hey, I did. I can understand you now! Wow!"

"Yay!" Ivy cried, grabbing both of Holly's hands and spinning her around in a crazy little jig. "That's amazing!"

Peppermint Bark joined in the dance, leaping up to try to lick both girls—and Chris, too, when he joined in. "It's a Christmas miracle!" Chris exclaimed. "My sister is almost normal again!"

"Oh, please." Holly gave him a shove as she continued to dance. "Like you have any idea what's normal, you weirdo."

She was just kidding, but she saw her brother's face fall. He stopped dancing and turned away.

"Hey," she said, feeling bad. "Listen, Chris—"

Before she could go on, Ivy poked her hard in the shoulder. "Heads up," Ivy hissed. "Mr. Brooks is up there!"

Holly followed her friend's gaze. Poinsettia Square was less than half a block away. Sure enough, Mr. Brooks was visible at the edge of it, waving his arms to direct some people who were carrying around tables and stuff. He seemed busy right then, but if he turned and saw them . . .

"Grab that dog's leash and let's get out of here," Holly told her brother sharply. "We can figure out what to do when we're somewhere else."

13

Jingle All the Way

Chris walked a little behind the girls as they hurried down the block and around the corner. He couldn't believe Holly had been so mean—and just when he was starting to think she was getting back to normal!

I should have known better, he told himself glumly. *As long as Ivy is around, Holly doesn't care about me at all.*

"Okay, this should be far enough." Ivy stopped in front of a pizza place with a **CLOSED FOR CHRISTMAS** sign on the front door. "Mr. Brooks probably won't leave Poinsettia Square until the festival is over tonight."

"Yeah." Holly giggled. "He's having too much fun bossing around the volunteers—like my dad."

Ivy giggled too. "Better him than us!"

"Whatever," Chris broke in. "Let's just figure out where to search next, okay? Peppermint Bark, do you have any ideas?"

The little dog wagged his tail. "Um, not really," he barked. "Except maybe we should have lunch, or at least a snack? I'm kind of hungry."

Chris's stomach grumbled. He realized none of them had eaten anything since those smoothies several hours earlier. "Okay," he said. "But let's make it quick."

He looked around. This block held not only the pizza place, but several other restaurants and shops. Normally this part of town was bustling with shoppers and diners, but today it was deserted.

Holly was looking around too. "Where are we supposed to get food on Christmas Day?" she said. "Everything's closed."

"Not everything," Ivy said. "Jingle Junction is just a few blocks away."

"What's Jingle Junction?" Peppermint Bark perked up his ears. "That sounds Christmasy!"

Chris realized his furry friend was right. "Jingle

Junction is the holiday market," he told Peppermint Bark. "It's open all day on Christmas. There are food stalls, places to shop, and even a Santa Station, where kids can thank Santa for their gifts and start making requests for next year."

"Santa's there?" Peppermint Bark cried.

"Not the real one," Chris said.

"Yeah." Holly laughed. "Nobody would mistake skinny Principal Gonzalez as the real Santa! His belly always looks super lumpy and fake."

Ivy shrugged. "Maybe he's trying to look more like St. Nicholas, the old saint who some people think was the original Santa. He was actually pretty skinny, since he gave most of his food to the poor."

Chris glanced at Peppermint Bark. "Is the real Santa Claus skinny?"

The little dog barked out a laugh. "No way! Mrs. Claus keeps trying to get him to exercise more. But when he laughs, his belly still shakes like a bowl full of jelly!"

"Whatever," Holly said. "Let's go to Jingle Junction. It's super Christmasy, and it has food. Two birds with one stone, right?"

Jingle Junction was the most magical place Peppermint Bark had ever seen! It took up most of Poinsettia Park, a large green space near Poinsettia Valley University. The market was ringed with a chainlink fence made to look friendly and festive with lights and garlands of greenery woven through it and giant ornaments hanging everywhere. The sound system played Christmas songs, and people hummed or sang along as they hurried in and out through the wide entrance arch, which looked as though it were made out of giant candy canes.

"Just like the real North Pole!" Peppermint Bark cried. "Our gates look sort of like that."

"Really? Cool." Ivy looked impressed. "Wow, it's crowded!"

Peppermint Bark had to agree. He jumped aside as a giggling toddler wearing a Santa cap raced past.

"Sleigh, Mama!" the toddler cried, pointing at a stall set up right outside the gate. Several baby strollers were parked there, all of them festooned with ribbons or garlands. There were shopping carts, too, including one that was decorated to look like a smaller version of Santa's sleigh.

"Nice workmanship," Peppermint Bark barked, stepping closer to take a look. "That would probably fool the average reindeer."

The toddler's eyes went wide. "Doggy, Mama!" he cried. "Doggy talk!"

"Yes, yes." The child's mother shot Peppermint Bark a slightly suspicious look as she hurried forward and picked up the toddler. "Stay away from the doggy, sweetie." She turned to the teenage girl running the cart-and-stroller stand. "I'd like to rent one of the strollers, please."

The toddler's mother handed a small slip of green paper to the girl. Then the mom took a stroller, strapped the toddler in, and hurried through the gate, pushing him along.

The kids had been watching the toddler too. "Bet he's going to talk to Santa," Ivy said.

"Yeah." Holly smiled. "I used to love coming here when I was little! One year we came the week before Christmas and I asked Santa for a pony that looked like a unicorn." She laughed. "I was so bummed when there wasn't one waiting for me under the tree!"

"I love unicorns!" Ivy exclaimed. Then she shrugged, looking slightly sad. "I've never talked to Santa, though." She glanced at Peppermint Bark. "Not even a fake one. They always had one at the mall in my old hometown, but we were usually out of the country when he was there."

"Well, you'll love Jingle Junction." Holly put an arm around her friend's shoulders. "I'll even take you to sit on Santa's lap if you want."

"No — there's no time for that," Chris blurted out.

Peppermint Bark tilted his head at Chris. The boy sounded awfully tense! Sure, Peppermint Bark was worried about getting home in time too. But it was Christmas!

"There's always time for Santa," he told the boy.

Chris just shrugged. "Anyway, we should hurry," he said. "Let's go in."

He led the way forward. Peppermint Bark followed — and almost bumped into his friend's legs when Chris stopped abruptly.

"Oh no!" Chris exclaimed, pointing to a sign hanging beside the arched entrance. "No dogs allowed!"

14

Merry Christmas Baby

"Now what?" Ivy said.

Holly sighed. Okay, so it was cool that Santa's puppy was right here in Poinsettia, and there were portals to the North Pole, and all the rest of it. It was as if all the stuff Ivy was always talking about had suddenly started coming to life! And Holly definitely wanted to help Peppermint Bark get home. Still, she was getting tired of wandering around outside. Her fingers were cold inside her cute purple gloves, and she could hardly feel her toes.

"No biggie. Peppermint Bark can stay outside," she

said. "We'll run in, grab some food, and take a look around for portals."

"No!" Chris said. "We can't leave him out here alone."

Ivy nodded. "True. Leash laws, remember?"

"Fine." Holly still didn't see the problem. "So Chris can stay out here with him."

"Forget it." Chris unzipped his puffer coat. "I'll just sneak him in under my jacket."

Holly laughed. "Really? Talk about a belly like a bowl full of jelly . . ."

"Yeah, I don't think that'll work," Ivy said. "He's too big. Somebody will notice, and then we'll get in trouble."

"So what?" Chris sounded stubborn, like always when he didn't get his way. Holly had seen it a zillion times.

She opened her mouth to respond. But just then, out of the corner of her eye, she saw someone—or something?—dash out from behind a dumpster and disappear into the crowds moving through the archway. Whatever—whoever—was moving too fast for Holly to get a good look, but it was red and green and small and looked an awful lot like whatever she'd seen in the bushes earlier . . .

"Hols?" Ivy prompted.

Holly blinked, telling herself she was seeing things. Or maybe just going nuts. Hanging out with fantasy-loving Ivy and believes-anything Chris was going to her head.

"So if somebody catches us sneaking a dog into the Junction, they might banish us for the rest of the day," she told the two of them. "And that means no looking for portals in there."

"And no lunch," Peppermint Bark added, licking his chops. "I think I smell Christmas cookies."

Chris crossed his arms, looking more stubborn than ever. "I'm not waiting out here. And neither is Peppermint Bark."

"So what do you suggest?" Holly challenged her brother, fed up. "Listen, if you're going to be like that, Ivy and I have better things to do. Right, Ives?"

Ivy didn't respond. When Holly looked over, her friend was staring off into space. For a second Holly wondered if Ivy had seen whatever Holly had just seen.

But no. Holly recognized that look. Ivy always got all spacy like that when she was thinking hard—"lost in her own imagination," some of their teachers called it. Holly poked her on the arm.

"Huh?" Ivy blinked at her. "Hey, I think I have an idea . . ."

A few minutes later, the kids were putting Ivy's plan into action. Chris had been a little dubious when she'd first told him and Holly about it. But he couldn't think of a better way to get Peppermint Bark into the market, so he'd just crossed his fingers and hoped it would work.

First they'd pooled their money, using part of it to rent a baby stroller. Then Ivy had dashed into the market to buy baby clothes—she'd remembered that the high school home-ec classes made items and sold them there.

"This stuff seemed like it would be around the right size," she said, tossing a dress and bonnet to Chris. "Here—see if you can get them on him."

Peppermint Bark looked confused. "I have to wear clothes?" he said. "But I'm a dog."

"No, you're not," Holly told him. "For the next few minutes, you're a baby. Got it?"

Ivy smiled and nodded. "I got the idea from fairy tales," she explained. "There are tricky disguises in lots of them. Like in 'Little Red Riding Hood,' when the wolf dresses up in a nightgown and bonnet and fools Red into thinking he's her grandmother. Remember?"

"Yeah, I guess." Chris unbuttoned the baby dress. "Come on, buddy. Let's see if this fits."

Peppermint Bark looked doubtful as Chris buttoned the dress around the dog's stout, furry body. It was a little tight at the top, but it was long enough to cover his back paws and tail.

"His front paws are sticking out," Holly said. "That'll give him away." She reached over to tweak the lace on the sleeves.

"So will his face!" Ivy giggled. "Put the bonnet on, Chris."

"Okay." Chris held up the bonnet.

But Peppermint Bark backed away. "That goes on my head?" he protested. "But I won't be able to see!"

"And nobody will be able to see you, either," Holly said. "That's kind of the point, okay?"

Peppermint Bark still looked wary. Chris scratched him behind the ear. "It's okay, pal," he said. "We'll be right with you. Please let me put it on?"

Peppermint Bark wagged his tail, which made the dress wave back and forth. "Well . . . okay, Chris."

Chris smiled at the trusting look in the puppy's soft brown eyes. He was really going to miss Peppermint Bark . . . But no. He wasn't going to think about that now.

"Hold still, okay?" he said. Then he tied on the bonnet. It completely hid the little dog's face and ears. Only the tip of his dark nose stuck out.

Holly studied him, looking a bit uncertain. "If anyone looks too closely . . ."

"They won't," Ivy assured her. "It's, like, a thing. Scientists have done studies about it. People see a stroller and a bonnet, they expect a baby. They won't look hard enough to notice anything else."

Holly shrugged. "If you say so."

"She just did, right?" Chris patted the seat of the stroller. "Hop in, Peppermint Bark."

Soon they were entering Jingle Junction. Holly pushed the stroller, while Chris and Ivy walked on either side of it to help hide Peppermint Bark from view. Most people hurried right past without so much as glancing in their direction.

Inside, the market was crowded. The Fa-La-La

Fudge stall was giving out free samples, so there were tons of people trying to push their way up to the counter. Chris and the others skirted the mob, heading farther in toward the other food stalls.

Chris glanced down at Peppermint Bark. He was wiggling a little. "Doing okay, buddy?" Chris whispered.

"Sure, Chris," the little dog barked softly.

A passing woman paused, glancing toward the stroller with surprise. Ivy stepped forward to block the lady's view, smiling widely. "You might not want to get too close," Ivy said. "My—uh—little cousin has the croup." She coughed into her hand to demonstrate.

"Oh dear." The woman nodded sympathetically. "Hope he's feeling better soon, poor little thing."

"Thanks." Ivy kept smiling until the woman moved on, then let out a relieved breath in a big whoosh.

"Good save, Ives," Holly whispered.

Chris nodded, for once glad to have Ivy along. "Yeah, that was quick thinking. But let's keep moving. The sooner we get some food and take a look around for portals, the sooner we can get out of here."

He was feeling a little tense. Normally Jingle Junction was one of his favorite spots in town. Today? It felt as if he and Peppermint Bark were outlaws trying to blend in at a sheriffs' convention.

Finally they reached Sugarplum Square, where most of the food vendors were set up. Chris waited with the stroller behind a large humming generator at one of the stalls while the girls bought food for all of them.

Peppermint Bark gobbled down the hot dog they brought him, then ate several Christmas cookies.

"Mmm, delicious!" he barked. "These cookies are almost as good as the ones Mrs. Claus bakes!"

Chris licked mustard off his fingers. Then he re-tied Peppermint Bark's bonnet, which he'd pushed back so the dog could eat. "Okay, let's take a quick look around for portals," Chris said as he pulled his gloves back on. "Peppermint Bark, you can still smell from behind that bonnet, right?"

"Sure, Chris," Peppermint Bark said. His nose twitched. "Everything here smells great! But I don't smell home yet."

"Let's check out the Santa Station," Ivy said. "That's the most Christmasy part of the whole Junction, right? So that's probably where a portal would be if there's one here."

"Makes sense," Holly agreed. "It's this way."

They wound their way through the crowds toward the back of the park. They had to swing wide to avoid a herd of little kids clustered around a candy stand giving out free Christmas lollipops. As Chris and the girls moved past them, Chris felt something bounce off his leg.

"Hey," he blurted out in surprise. He glanced down just in time to spot a weird-looking little kid in a striped cap disappear into the mob at the lollipop stand.

Ivy glanced over at Chris. "What's wrong?" she asked.

Chris stared after the kid—or had it been a kid? Something didn't seem quite right . . .

Before he could say anything, a gangly boy with dark hair rushed up to them. Chris recognized him as one of his sister's classmates. "Holly, Ivy!" the boy exclaimed. "Yo, what's up?"

"Oh, hi, Hassan." Holly shot a worried look at Chris and Ivy. "Not much. Listen, we're kind of in a hurry, so . . ."

But the boy was already staring down at the stroller. "Who's the baby?" he asked. "Your parents decide you needed another brother?" Hassan laughed loudly at his own joke.

"No, he's with me," Ivy said quickly, grabbing the handles of the stroller from Holly. "My little cousin. But he's sleeping, so don't wake him up, okay?"

Hassan leaned over to peer past Ivy, confusion creeping over his face. "Is he okay?" he said. "He looks a little . . ."

"Oh, is that the time?" Ivy said loudly. "Listen, we have to go. Merry Christmas, Hassan!"

"Merry Christmas!" Holly and Chris chorused, crowding along beside the stroller as Ivy pushed it away as fast as she could in the busy market.

"Merry Christmas!" Peppermint Bark barked.

Chris froze. Hassan looked more confused than ever, staring from the stroller to the kids and back again.

Holly reached into her coat pocket and whipped out her phone. "Do you like my new ring tone?" she asked Hassan cheerfully. "It sounds just like a real dog, right?"

Hassan's face cleared. He laughed. "Yeah, cool," he said. "Mine sounds like an airplane taking off."

"Is that Dad calling for us to come home?" Chris asked his sister. "We should go."

He didn't let out the breath he was holding until Hassan was out of sight in the crowds behind them.

"That was close!" Chris hissed at the girls. "We really need to get out of here."

"Okay, but we're almost at the Santa Station," Holly said.

"Yeah." Ivy pushed the stroller around a stand selling Christmas-themed throw pillows. "We'll just take a quick look and then leave, okay?"

15

Santa Station Altercation

Peppermint Bark tried to do as Chris said and stay hidden inside his disguise. But when the little dog heard a loud "Ho ho ho!" from somewhere nearby, he couldn't resist peeking out from inside the bonnet.

"Careful!" Chris leaned down and tweaked the bonnet back over Peppermint Bark's eyes. "Someone will see you."

Peppermint Bark was disappointed. He wished he could see more. Because the glimpse he'd caught of the Santa Station was amazing! Mountains of snow dotted with twinkling lights surrounded a festive platform. An enormous golden chair sat at the center with a jolly red-suited fellow ho-ho-ho-ing as he bounced a tiny pink-cheeked child on his knee. Brightly wrapped packages were piled on either side of the chair, and people in peppermint-striped sweaters and jaunty green hats were keeping eager hordes of children calm as they waited in line for their turn . . .

But even though he couldn't see with the bonnet over his face, Peppermint Bark could still smell. And there were *lots* of smells here! Some were easy to pick out — like the strawberry ice cream smeared over a toddler's face, or the soiled diaper on a nearby baby. Other aromas swirled together into one big, happy holiday hodgepodge. Peppermint Bark thought he caught a whiff of cinnamon, and then the breeze changed and he smelled candy canes, then spruce branches . . .

His nose twitched as he took in all the tantalizing scents, searching for the one he was looking for — gingerbread and pinecones, just like home.

Suddenly he felt the stroller jerk. A second later, a high-pitched voice rang out. "This way, please!"

Peppermint Bark couldn't hear that well through the bonnet, but something about that voice seemed familiar . . . The little dog sniffed again, then blinked. Hold on — was that the smell? The scent of a portal?

Wait—and there was something else, too—another very familiar odor . . .

"No!" Ivy exclaimed. "Stop it—we're not trying to get in line."

The stroller jerked again, this time in the opposite direction. Peppermint Bark stiffened, trying not to let his disguise slip. But he could feel the bonnet sliding off his left ear . . .

🌲

Chris had been looking around for portals, so he wasn't watching the stroller when Ivy cried out in alarm. When he looked that way, he saw that two tiny kids in elf costumes had appeared out of nowhere and were trying to get between her and the stroller.

Uh-oh! What if they looked down and noticed Peppermint Bark in there? Chris tried to jump forward to help Ivy get away from the kids, but his path was blocked by a pair of little girls holding hands who had just stopped to stare wide-eyed at Santa. Chris danced from side to side, trying to find a way past them, but the whole area was pretty crowded. To his left, a broad-shouldered dad was snapping photos with his phone.

To Chris's right, several teenagers were jostling one another and joking about asking Santa for a new car. Meanwhile, the two elf-kids were trying to herd the stroller toward the line of little kids awaiting their turns on Santa's lap.

"Hey, stop—she already told you we don't want to get in line!" Chris yelled, realizing that the elf-kids must be Santa assistants trying to keep the crowd organized.

Chris finally got past the little girls and ran forward, trying to grab the side of the stroller to stop the elf-kids from hustling it farther away. Ivy was still clutching the handles, but she seemed distracted, staring at the assistants with her mouth open in surprise. Before Chris could help, the stroller rolled off into the crowd, with Ivy barely holding on.

"No, no, no, children. You have to go this way." The female Santa assistant's voice was high-pitched and singsongy.

"Yes, yes," the second one said. "It's very important. Very, very, very important."

Holly pushed her way toward them, looking annoyed. "Listen, you have to—"

She was interrupted by a loud woman's voice from somewhere close by: "This way, children!" the voice called out. "Everyone from the number seven bus trip, come this way if you want to talk to Santa!"

"Tourists," Holly said.

Chris nodded. Poinsettia was famous for its Christmas spirit. Every year, lots of people came from other towns near and far to join in the holiday celebration. "Don't you mean ho-ho-holidayers?" he joked, remembering the name his sister had invented for the visitors.

Holly laughed. "I forgot about that!" she said, grinning at Chris.

Just then a new stampede of little kids arrived at the Santa Station. "Santa!" a bright-eyed girl shrieked, hurling herself forward.

"Santa, Santa!" the rest of the little kids yelled, pushing and shoving as they tried to get to the front of the line.

"Whoa!" Chris said as one of the little boys crashed into him and went sprawling. "Careful, buddy! You don't want to get hurt."

He reached down and helped the little kid to his feet. The boy immediately raced away again. "Santa!" he screamed excitedly.

The boy's father hurried past. "Thanks, son," he

called to Chris over his shoulder. "He's a little over-whelmed. Santa, you know . . ."

"Sure, anytime," Chris said, though the man was al-ready disappearing into the crowd.

"Come on, we have to catch up to Ivy," Holly re-minded Chris, jumping from one foot to the other as she looked for a way through the crowd. "This is crazy!"

Chris nodded, stepping aside as a wild-eyed little girl with a half-licked lollipop in one hand hurtled past. Holly was right. They had to get to Peppermint Bark!

Over the little kids' heads, Chris could see Ivy and the stroller. The Santa assistants were still herding them along, taking Peppermint Bark farther away with every step. Suddenly Chris noticed something else.

"They're not guiding the stroller toward the line waiting for Santa," he said.

Holly's eyes widened. "You're right—I think they're taking it toward the emergency exit." She pointed at a door in the chainlink fence just beyond the fake snow wall encircling the Santa Station. "What's up with that?"

Chris wasn't sure. Had the assistants noticed that Peppermint Bark was a dog? Were they kicking him out of the Junction? Chris glanced around, hoping to spy a way through the throngs of kids.

Instead, he noticed something else—a shimmering spot on the fake snow wall nearby. "A portal!" he blurted out.

Holly turned and saw it too. "I knew there'd be one here!" she cried. "Come on, we have to get to Peppermint Bark!"

"Yeah." Was Chris imagining it, or was the shimmering spot shrinking? He thought back to the way the one at the post office had blinked out of sight. "And fast!"

They tried to speed up. But there seemed to be more little kids arriving by the second to block their path. And the stroller was moving faster by now—Ivy still had one hand on the handle, but the two Santa assistants were pushing it along as fast as they could.

"Hurry, hurry!" one of them cried out in his high-pitched voice. "We have to hurry!"

"You know, there's something weird about those assistants," Holly commented. "They're not dressed like most of the others."

Chris wasn't sure why his sister was always so worried about clothes and stuff lately. "Who cares?" he said breathlessly, dodging a little kid waving a lollipop in each hand. "This way!"

"No, I'm serious," Holly said as she followed. "Don't they look weird to you? They're really tiny, for one thing. They're definitely not adults, but they didn't really sound like kids, either . . ."

"Whatever." Chris was hardly listening. Ivy and the stroller were almost at the snow wall by then. If he could just get to Peppermint Bark before that portal closed . . . Chris pushed forward, causing a little kid to squawk in protest. "Sorry, excuse me," Chris mumbled. "Coming through . . ."

Up ahead near the stroller, several little kids were stampeding in from the other direction. "Santa!" a boy cried. "Me first, me first!"

The boy charged forward . . . and tripped over the stroller's front wheel! The kid went flying. Ivy lunged for the stroller, but it was too late. It tipped over, spilling Peppermint Bark onto the ground on his back. The baby gown was scrunched up, revealing the little dog's furry paws, and the bonnet was half off . . .

"Oh no!" Chris exclaimed. "We have to get over there before someone sees him!"

16

Dash Away, Dash Away, Dash Away All . . .

Peppermint Bark's legs were tangled in his silly dress, and the bonnet was askew. He was struggling to turn himself upright when he felt someone pick him up.

"Don't bark," Ivy whispered in his ear as she pressed Peppermint Bark against her soft ivy-embroidered scarf. "Keep your face hidden."

Peppermint Bark leaned against her, doing his best to hide his snout from view in the folds of the scarf. Even so, he could see a little bit of what was happening around him. Young kids were running in every direction. The Santa helper he'd caught a glimpse of earlier was still sitting on his golden chair nearby.

And there—just behind the Santa helper—was the portal the little dog had smelled! Peppermint Bark gasped, but before he could bark to let Ivy know, the portal swirled shut!

Oh no! he thought, his heart sinking. *It must be getting late. Because there goes another one . . .*

There was no more time to worry about it. Ivy was trying to make her way toward Chris and Holly, but it was slow going thanks to the excited children running around everywhere.

Suddenly Ivy froze in place. For a second Peppermint Bark was confused. Weren't they trying to escape?

Then a voice rang out: "Settle down, children!"

Peppermint Bark knew that voice. It was the man they'd seen earlier—Mr. Brooks. The kids didn't seem to like him, though Peppermint Bark wasn't sure why.

He peeked carefully over Ivy's scarf at Mr. Brooks, who looked stern. "It's a good thing I came here to pick up more candy canes for the festival!" the man blustered, waving his hands in the air. His mustache quivered with indignation. "What chaos! Parents, control your children or we'll have to shut down the Santa Station!"

"Uh-oh," Ivy whispered, her voice so soft that even

Peppermint Bark, with his keen ears, barely heard her. "We have to get out of here before he sees you."

She held Peppermint Bark even more tightly. Peppermint Bark snuggled against her, turning his face all the way in. He hoped his furry ear wasn't sticking out the top of the bonnet . . .

A moment later he heard the soft clink of metal. Finally Ivy stopped moving.

"That was close!" Chris's breathless voice exclaimed a few seconds later.

"Yeah," Holly added. "Good thing there's no alarm on the emergency exit."

Peppermint Bark didn't have a chance to wonder what that meant. Because just then, Ivy flung him away.

"Yikes!" he cried—but then he felt Chris's familiar arms grab him around the middle.

"Oof!" Chris grunted, then set Peppermint Bark gently on the ground. "Whoa, Ivy. You could have warned me you were going to throw him at me!"

"Whatever." Ivy's voice sounded shaky. When Peppermint Bark peeked out from under the bonnet, which had slipped down to cover one eye, he saw that the girl's face had gone bright red.

"Listen," he barked. "I have to tell you guys something . . ."

But Chris and Holly were both staring at Ivy now. "What's wrong?" Holly asked her friend. "You look weird."

"Guys," Peppermint Bark tried again.

But then he pricked up his ears. Something rustled in the leaves at the edge of the park. When he looked that way, he caught a glimpse of a striped stocking cap.

He was right! The other smell he'd recognized . . . they'd come for him!

"Stop!" he barked, racing off after the stocking cap. "Here I am! Wait for me!"

Chris was startled when Peppermint Bark took off howling with excitement. At first Chris couldn't make out any clear words in the excited little dog's woofs. But then he heard it — "Elves! Elves! Elves!"

"Where's he going?" Holly cried.

"I'm not sure." Chris was already running after the dog. "But we've got to catch him!"

As soon as Chris emerged from the woods at the

edge of the park, he could see what had set off the little dog. The girls were on Chris's heels, and they saw too.

"It's the Serafini triplets!" Ivy exclaimed.

"Yeah." Chris sped up. "Peppermint Bark must think they're real elves from the North Pole."

The Serafini triplets were six years old and never seemed to stop moving. Their favorite way to get around town was on their matching red scooters, which they were riding now.

"Peppermint Bark!" Chris yelled. "Wait—slow down!"

"I'll get him." Holly pushed past her brother. She put her head down and started sprinting as fast as she could—which was pretty fast. Soon Chris and Ivy fell way behind.

Chris skidded to a stop on the corner of Turtledove Street, breathing hard. Ivy stopped too.

"She's really fast," Ivy said. "I think she'll catch him."

"I hope so." Chris crossed his fingers as he watched his sister sprint after Peppermint Bark. The triplets veered across the street, and the dog had to slow down to make the turn after them. Holly took a big leap, landing with one foot on the end of the makeshift leash.

With a yelp, Peppermint Bark came to an abrupt

halt. "Let me go, let me go!" he barked. "I have to catch those elves!"

Chris rushed to catch up. "They're not really elves," he called to Peppermint Bark. "They're just regular kids —like us."

"What?" The little white dog didn't seem to hear him. He strained against his collar, trying to pull free of Holly.

"They're not elves!" Chris finally reached the little dog. The boy fell to his knees and grabbed his friend, turning Peppermint Bark's head so he could look into his eyes. "Listen! We know those kids. They're not elves, okay?"

Ivy had caught up by then too. "What if they are, though?" she said, staring after the Serafini triplets. "Maybe they got stuck here last Christmas—just like Peppermint Bark!"

"No." Peppermint Bark shook his head. He'd finally stopped struggling, though he was still peering down the street after the triplets. "No elves ride with Santa. And none were missing. They were all at the North Pole making toys this year. I know—it's part of my job to keep track of them."

"That's what I'm trying to tell you," Chris said with

a sigh. "Those kids you were chasing? Definitely not real elves."

"But I smelled them!" Peppermint Bark licked his nose, looking confused. "Back by the Santa Station—I smelled the portal, and there was something else that smelled like home too. Elves! Real ones. I didn't see them, but I smelled them—and then I spotted those striped stocking caps . . ."

He collapsed on the sidewalk, ears drooping and tail still. "It's okay, buddy." Chris stroked the puppy's soft white fur. "We'll get you home."

"But the portals keep closing," Peppermint Bark said sadly. "What if we're already too late? It's starting to get dark."

Chris realized the little dog was right. Twilight came quickly this time of year, and the shadows of the trees and buildings were growing longer and longer. The twinkling stars dangling from all the street lamps were blinking on, and the growing darkness made it easier to see the holiday lights strung on the bushes and buildings nearby.

"Don't worry, Peppermint Bark," Holly said. "We'll get you back to the North Pole."

"Thanks." Peppermint Bark sighed. "I hope so. I

miss it already. The elves, the reindeer, and of course Santa . . ."

Chris bit his lip, worried by how sad the little dog looked. As much as he hated the thought of Peppermint Bark leaving—of maybe never seeing him ever again—Chris knew it wasn't fair to wish he could stay. He had to help his new friend find a way home—no matter what.

17

Over the Chainlink and Through the Woods

"Where'd they go?" Juniper sounded frantic as she clutched her striped cap. "We had him! We almost had him! Aargh!"

Happy looked around the busy Santa Station. A stern-looking older man with white hair was shouting and waving his arms around, herding the hordes of human children into tidy lines.

"I don't know," Happy said, tilting his cap back for a better view. "These humans are awfully tall—I lost track of him once that girl grabbed him."

"We're too late, anyhow—the portal is closed." Juniper scowled, glancing up at the fake snow wall nearby.

Then she gulped. "Wait—the portal is closed! How are we supposed to get home, let alone rescue Peppermint Bark?"

"I'm sure there must be lots of portals in a town this Christmasy. All we have to do is find another one —one that's still open." Happy smiled, trying to make Juniper feel better. "At least now we know for sure that Peppermint Bark is nearby . . ."

Juniper glared at him. "This is no time to be so cocoa-mug-half-full about everything," she growled. "We're running out of time, and now we might be trapped here ourselves!"

But Happy hardly heard her. He tilted his head, the tips of his long ears quivering. "Did you hear that?" he said. "Barking!" He pointed to the chainlink fence behind the Santa Station. "We're too far away to hear what he's saying, but I think Peppermint Bark is out there!"

"There's a door—let's go!" Juniper scurried toward the gate. But when she tried to grab the latch to open it, she couldn't quite reach. "Gah! Why is everything here so tall?" she cried.

"Never mind—let's climb." Happy grabbed a strand of garland that was woven through the metal fence.

Juniper followed, the two of them scrambling up, up, up . . .

"Hey, Mama, look!" a child's voice cried. "Those elves are climbing the fence!"

"Hush, baby," a woman replied. "It's almost your turn, all right?"

When Happy glanced over his shoulder, he spotted a little girl with cornrows grinning and pointing at him and Juniper. Beside the girl, a woman was peering toward the front of the Santa Station line, tapping her foot impatiently.

Then Happy gasped as he felt a hand grab him and haul him up over the top of the fence. "Hurry up," Juniper said. "We'll never catch up to Peppermint Bark if you hang there goggling at the humans all day."

"Sorry, Juniper." Happy quickly scrambled down the far side of the fence, landing in a pretty, forested area.

"There!" Juniper cried as a faint bark drifted through the trees. "They're heading that way," she said, pointing.

As the two of them raced through the park and out onto the street, Happy couldn't stop thinking about everything they'd seen since arriving in Poinsettia. Why had he been so scared to leave the North Pole? The rest of the world was amazing! There were buildings, lots of them, a few even taller than the snow castle. There were giant versions of the toy cars he'd built many times, which moved with a funny growling sound. And of course, there were the people—more people than he could have imagined. No wonder the elves had to make so many toys every year!

"Where could those meddling kids be taking Peppermint Bark, anyway?" Juniper grumbled as she ran, dodging streetlights and parked cars. "Why are they trying to stop us from taking him home?"

"I don't know." Happy put on a burst of speed to catch up as they rounded the corner onto another deserted street. "Maybe we should ask them." Suddenly he thought of something else. "Oh! Maybe they don't know that's what we're doing—we should tell them!"

"No!" Juniper stopped so abruptly that Happy bumped into her before he could stop himself. "We can't tell them why we're here. We promised Mrs. Claus we'd keep our identity a secret, remember?"

"Oh." Happy scratched his head. That did sound familiar. "Okay. But she also wants us to do whatever it takes to get Peppermint Bark home before the gates close. Maybe we need to . . ."

He let his words trail off. Juniper was already running again and pulling away fast. He raced after her, wondering why she was so sure they couldn't trust the kids who had Peppermint Bark. After all, she didn't know any more about humans or their world than Happy did. He'd seen those kids up close—he and Juniper had spied on them from some bushes, and then again at the Jingle Junction. And he'd taken a good look at the dark-haired girl who'd been pushing Peppermint Bark around in the baby stroller. She had looked nice —they all had. And Santa always said that human kids loved everything about Christmas. What harm could it do to at least try explaining why the elves wanted Peppermint Bark?

Then again, Juniper had already decided what to do. And she probably knew best—she usually did. That was why she made such a good Head Elf.

"Hey, wait for me!" Happy cried, speeding up again as Juniper disappeared around another corner.

Chris wandered along Silverbell Street, trailing the others, watching Peppermint Bark. He couldn't believe this was happening. They'd already spotted two portals —just moments too late. He'd promised his new friend that he'd help him get home, but what if Chris couldn't keep that promise?

"There's an extra-fancy one," Ivy said, interrupting his worries. She pointed to a large Victorian house with candles in every window and icicle lights on every post and gable.

Chris nodded, but he was starting to wonder if this was a waste of time. "Yeah," he said. "Anything, buddy?"

Peppermint Bark sniffed, then shook his head. The four of them had been wandering along the streets near the center of town for almost an hour, looking for portals around the most festively decorated houses and businesses. The light was fading rapidly as the hour grew later, and Poinsettia looked beautiful as white and silver and multihued lights glowed everywhere. Normally this was one of Chris's favorite times of the holiday season. But today he couldn't enjoy it.

Holly was leading the way as they rounded a corner. "Check it out," she said. "Carolers!"

Peppermint Bark looked up. "Oh, I've heard about those!" he exclaimed. "Santa says they're people who sing beautiful Christmas songs, just like the elves back home." He looked a little wistful. "I do miss their singing . . ."

"You don't have to," Holly said. "Just listen!"

Peppermint Bark tilted his head, his tongue hanging out and his breath showing as little white puffs in the cold December air. Chris listened too. The carolers stood in front of a house halfway down the block, singing "The Twelve Days of Christmas."

"This is one of my favorites," Chris said. For a second he smiled, letting the music wash over him—along with a serious dose of Christmas spirit. But it faded when he looked at Peppermint Bark's wistful face. Unlike in the song, they didn't have twelve days of Christmas to get Santa's puppy back home. Just one day—today. And the sun was already setting . . .

Happy peeked out from behind a parked car on Eggnog Street. "They're still walking this way," he whispered to Juniper. "Where do you think they're going?"

"Who cares?" Juniper said. "They've got Peppermint Bark—and we need to rescue him!" She shook her head. "Santa always made it sound as if all children are good and almost none are truly naughty."

"Yes." Happy nodded. "He says that's why we elves have to work so hard all year making toys. Because there are so many good girls and boys to give them to!"

"Right." Juniper shrugged, peeking out from their hiding spot herself. "But I'm starting to wonder . . ."

"What do you mean?" Happy pulled his cap lower on his face. Night was falling, and the air was sharp with cold and coming snow. He sniffed for it, his long nose wiggling. Yes, definitely—there would be snow soon.

Juniper wasn't thinking about snow. She watched Peppermint Bark and his human companions through narrowed eyes. "I think these children must be extremely naughty," she said. "Why else would they keep preventing us from taking Peppermint Bark home where he belongs? In any case, we should be able to grab him as they pass."

"Are you sure about the children being naughty?" Happy asked. "I was thinking about it, and they don't seem naughty—just, perhaps, a little confused. Maybe if we tried talking to them, like I was saying earlier . . ."

"Ahoy there—elves!" a man's voice interrupted. "What are you doing here? The final check of the parade floats is happening right now! I'm sure the other kids from your group are wondering what's keeping you, eh? Let's get you to Poinsettia Square posthaste."

Happy goggled up at a human man with a tidy white mustache. He looked sort of familiar—had they seen him before? Happy wasn't sure. All humans looked pretty much the same to him, other than the children, of course . . .

"No, no," Juniper began. "We're not . . ."

But it was too late. The man had already grabbed the elves by the collars of their spruce-green tunics and hustled them off across the street.

18

Festival Time

Holly was frustrated. So far this whole portal search had been a bust. And Holly hated failing at stuff. That was why she tried never to do it.

She dragged her feet as they followed the carolers down the block, where there was no sign of a portal. Just like the other places they'd checked—pretty much every Christmasy place in town. Well, every place except one big one . . .

"Look, guys." Holly stopped on the corner of Eggnog and Spruce Streets and turned to face the others. "There's one super Christmasy place we haven't searched yet. Poinsettia Square."

"The festival." Chris glanced at the big clock on the town hall. "It's supposed to be starting right around now."

"And it's probably the most Christmasy place in town," Ivy agreed. "Let's try it."

Chris looked worried. "But our families will be there—and our teachers, and neighbors, and everybody else we know." He shrugged. "How are we supposed to search with them all watching us?"

"Not to mention Mr. Brooks." Ivy glanced at Peppermint Bark worriedly. "He might not be thrilled to see you-know-who again."

Peppermint Bark wagged his tail. "You mean me, right?" he guessed. "Hey, but this festival place sounds really Christmasy! Just like the kind of spot where Santa likes to hide the portals!"

"See?" Holly said to Chris and Ivy, who both still looked worried. "It's worth a look. Because otherwise, we're kind of all out of ideas."

Chris couldn't stop thinking about how little time they had left to get Peppermint Bark home. And how hard it would be to sneak away from the festival once they got there. As in, impossible. Even if his parents didn't stop them, Mr. Brooks or Ivy's parents or some other well-meaning adult would insist the kids stay put.

Still, Holly was right—Poinsettia Square was definitely the most Christmasy place in town right now. "I guess it makes sense to check the festival," Chris said at last.

"Totally," Ivy agreed. "Like Hols says, it's pretty much the only place we haven't already looked." She glanced at Holly. "Can I borrow your phone to text my parents and let them know I'm heading to the festival? They're probably wondering where I am by now."

After Ivy sent her text, the kids and Peppermint Bark all turned to walk toward the square, which was about two blocks away. The streets around them were deserted—Chris figured that almost everyone in town was already at the festival.

As they turned the corner onto Noel Street, Peppermint Bark looked worried, but then he wagged his tail. "It's okay, I know you guys are trying your best," he said. "If there's no portal at this square place, I can just stay here with you until next Christmas."

Chris's heart jumped with hope. Peppermint Bark wanted to stay! It would be great—they could spend the whole year together. Peppermint Bark could sleep at the foot of his bed, and Chris could teach him to fetch a stick—or maybe a candy cane . . .

But Chris's hopes came crashing back to earth when Holly shook her head. "Wish you could, Peppermint Bark," she told the little dog. "But our dad's allergic, remember? He and Mom are planning to take you to the animal shelter first thing in the morning."

"Animal shelter?" Peppermint Bark tilted his head quizzically. "Is that like the stable where the reindeer sleep?"

"Not exactly," Holly said, as she and Ivy traded a look.

Chris gulped. "It's a nice place, though," he said. "The people there take really good care of the animals until someone adopts them."

"Yeah." Ivy paused to pick up a piece of tinsel that had blown off a nearby house. "I went there once to help my neighbor pick out a cat. The cages are really big, with soft beds in them and everything."

Peppermint Bark's tail drooped. "C-cages?" he said uncertainly.

Chris glared at Ivy. Why did she have to mention cages?

Then his eyes widened as an idea popped into his head. If he couldn't keep Peppermint Bark himself, maybe Ivy could be useful for once . . .

"You could take him!" Chris blurted out. He stopped short and turned to face the two girls. "Hey, Ivy, maybe Peppermint Bark could stay with you!"

"What? No!" Ivy said quickly. "I can't adopt him. Anyway, we'll probably find a portal at the festival."

"But what if we don't?" Chris put his hands on his hips. "He can't live with us because of Dad's allergies. But he could live with you! I bet your parents would say yes."

Holly nodded eagerly. "That's actually a good idea," she said to her friend. "Your mom and dad are so nice, I bet they'd be okay with it."

"No!" Ivy's cheeks had already been pink from the cold, but now they went bright red. "I don't want to." She shot an apologetic look at Peppermint Bark. "Sorry," she said softly, her words muffled as she tucked her chin into her scarf. "I—I mean, I just can't."

"But why not?" Holly looked perplexed. "You don't have allergies, you've got plenty of room and a nice yard . . ."

"Because I'm afraid of dogs, okay?" Ivy yelled.

Chris's jaw dropped. "You're what?"

Ivy shrugged, ducking her head so her long hair fell forward to hide her face. "I'm afraid of dogs," she said softly. "I always have been."

Holly frowned. "How did I not know this? I thought we were best friends!"

"We are." Ivy peered up through her hair. "I never told you because it never came up." She looked at Peppermint Bark again. "Well, not until today, anyway. And I still didn't say anything because I thought you'd think I was a wimp. I mean, you're not afraid of anything."

"Hmm." Holly didn't say anything else for a second. Chris could tell she was deciding whether to be mad or not.

Meanwhile Peppermint Bark stepped forward, gazing up at Ivy with his soft brown eyes. "It's okay, Ivy," he said. "I understand. And thank you for rescuing me at the Santa Station even though you were scared."

"You're welcome." Ivy smiled slightly. "It wasn't that bad, I guess. You're kind of okay for a dog. Maybe it would even be sort of nice having you stay with me for the year, but it won't work no matter what I think." She glanced at Holly. "My mom's cat hates all other animals, remember?"

"Oh, right. And most people, too," Holly said with a grimace. "She scratches me every time I try to pet her."

"Oh. Thanks anyway, Ivy." Peppermint Bark wagged his tail, then sighed. "Anyway, I'm sure everything will be fine. Even if I can't live with you guys, maybe a nice person will adopt me. Though of course I'll miss Santa terribly. And Mrs. Claus. And Happy and the other elves, and of course the reindeer . . ."

Chris didn't know what to say. Part of him still wished that Peppermint Bark could stay. But Chris could see how sad it made the little dog to think about being away from home for so long.

Just then the cold evening breeze turned, bringing a burst of music from the direction of the square, just a little more than a block away. The glow of lights was brighter as the sky grew darker, and Chris could see the top of the huge town Christmas tree above the buildings. The festival planning committee was in charge of stringing the giant fir with twinkling holiday lights, but all citizens and visitors were invited to hang their own ornaments to create a huge, cheerful hodgepodge of Christmas spirit.

It probably feels like that at the North Pole all the time, Chris realized. *No wonder Peppermint Bark wants to get back there!*

"Come on," Chris told the others, stepping toward the square. "All this stuff won't matter if we can find a portal, right? And what better place to hide one than at the Poinsettia Holiday Festival!"

Peppermint Bark brightened. "Right, Chris!" he barked. "Let's go!"

"What time is it?" Ivy asked.

Holly gritted her teeth. "You just asked me that, like, ten seconds ago!" But she glanced at her watch. "It's five after eight."

They were in Poinsettia Square, where the festival was in full swing. Up on the bandstand, the high school music director was waving his arms as an orchestra of musicians in Santa hats played a jaunty version of "Jingle Bells." People were watching, and a few were dancing. Others were talking or eating or wandering around or adding their ornaments to the huge tree in the center of the square. The cold night air was laced with the tantalizing scents of roasting chestnuts and hot cocoa, tamales and panettone and borscht, savory dumplings with fragrant Indian spices, sweet and spongy *bibingka* from the Philippines, Tunisian marzipan balls flavored with rose water, and many other delicious Christmas treats from all over the world.

Holly glanced at her brother. Chris was holding Peppermint Bark's leash again. "Smell anything?" Holly asked the little dog.

"Lots of things!" Peppermint Bark let his tongue loll out in a smile. "No portals yet, but I bet there's one here somewhere."

"Let's just hope it doesn't close before we find it," Ivy said. "Hey, Peppermint Bark, do you know if all the portals here will close at midnight? Or could one stay open until the last time zone on Earth finishes Christmas?"

Peppermint Bark shook his head. "I'm not sure," he said. "I never thought about it much before. As long as Santa knew how they worked, the rest of us didn't pay that much attention to the details."

"It's okay," Chris told him.

"No, it's not." Holly frowned. "We know some portals have already closed, so—" She cut herself off as she saw several familiar faces rushing their way.

"Hey, guys!" a girl from school named Rachel shrieked. "Merry Christmas!"

Hot on Rachel's heels were several of Holly and Ivy's other friends. The next few minutes passed in a flurry of hugs, followed by lots of excited chatter about Christmas gifts. Holly didn't pay much attention, other than smiling as the other girls oohed and aahed over her birthstone necklace.

She was still distracted by their quest. Did they have only until midnight? If so, that didn't give them much time . . .

Finally Rachel and the others moved on. Chris had been hanging back, playing invisible as he always seemed to do when Holly's friends were around. But now he stepped forward.

"Let's keep moving," he said. "I was thinking we should check the Scrooge dunking booth next . . ."

There was no portal at the dunking booth. But the Oumas were there. Mr. Ouma hurled white tennis balls at the target, hoping to dunk Mayor Morris—who was dressed as Scrooge from *A Christmas Carol*—into a tank full of fake snow. Mrs. Ouma was nearby, chatting with Chris and Holly's kindergarten teacher, who had retired a couple of years earlier.

"Oh, look!" Mrs. Kasabian called out in her quavering, singsong voice. "It's two of my favorite former students!" Leaning on her walker, she hobbled closer, then peered at Ivy through her thick glasses. "And who have we here?"

Holly forced a smile. Mrs. Kasabian was one of the friendliest people in town. She could talk all day, telling stories and asking question after question. That had made her a great kindergarten teacher, but it also meant that running into her could take up a lot of time — time they didn't have right now.

"Merry Christmas, Mrs. Kasabian," Chris said. "This is, um, our friend Ivy. She moved here last summer."

Holly glanced at her brother in surprise. Had he really just called Ivy a friend? Last Holly had heard, the two of them couldn't stand each other. Then again, a friendship between those two wouldn't even come close to being the strangest thing that had happened today . . .

"Lovely to meet you, Ivy." Mrs. Kasabian smiled. "So this is your first Christmas in Poinsettia, eh?"

"That's right," Ivy said in her usual polite way. "It's really fun! Everyone has so much Christmas spirit."

"Yes, they do!" Peppermint Bark barked. "It's great!"

Mrs. Kasabian blinked at the little dog. "Oh, how cute are you?" she said, bending down carefully to scratch Peppermint Bark on the head. "And look at your festive leash and collar—you're dressed for the season, too!" She chuckled. "When I was a girl, I had a lovely tabby cat who let me dress him up for Halloween . . ."

When the old lady finished the story about her cat, Holly smiled. She'd heard the story before, and it was actually one of her favorites. But her smile faded as she remembered that Peppermint Bark was counting on them. How could they escape without hurting Mrs. Kasabian's feelings?

Just then there was laughter from the dunk tank. Mr. Ouma's latest throw had finally sent Mayor Morris tumbling into the tank!

"Great shot, honey!" Mrs. Ouma called out.

The mayor climbed back onto his platform, sputtering and wiping fake snow out of his eyes, but smiling. "More like a lucky shot," he called.

"Oh yeah?" Mr. Ouma grinned, reaching for another "snowball." "We'll see about that, my friend . . ."

Suddenly Holly had an idea. "No, wait!" she called, hurrying over. "Mrs. K wants to try."

"What?" Mrs. Kasabian laughed. "Oh no, I don't think I'd be very good at that!"

"Sure you would." Holly pressed a ball into the old woman's hand. "You used to play softball when you were young — you told us about it lots of times. Besides, aren't you the one who always said the only way to lose is not to try?"

The old teacher's eyes brightened. "Well, I suppose you're right on both counts, Holly." Mrs. Kasabian patted her on the arm. "It's nice to know someone was listening to all those stories of mine . . ."

"Of course we were!" Chris exclaimed. "Your stories are great. And I bet you can dunk the mayor again, too!"

Mr. Ouma nodded. "If you do, I'll buy you a cocoa," he said. He winked at his wife and the other spectators. "Maybe I'll even buy one for Mayor Morris!"

"Well now, how could I say no to that?" Mrs. Kasabian said. "All right, here goes nothing . . ."

As the old woman stepped forward, Holly bent to whisper to Peppermint Bark. "Okay, I saw what happened earlier when you wagged your tail at Mr. Brooks and made him go nice all of a sudden. So I know you have, like, North Pole magic or whatever. Can you do anything to help here?"

Peppermint Bark wagged his tail. "I think so . . ."

He trotted forward, stopping right next to Mrs. Kasabian's walker. As she tossed the snowball, he wagged his tail again, and the sound of jingle bells floated through the air, blending with the music from the bandstand. The adults didn't seem to hear it, but the snowball sped up and hit the target hard enough to send Mayor Morris back into the tank of snow!

"Awesome!" Holly cheered, as Chris let out a whoop and Ivy pumped her fist. Peppermint Bark wagged his tail and jumped around, celebrating with the humans.

Mr. Ouma extended an arm to Mrs. Kasabian. "A deal is a deal," he said with a smile. "Let's get that cocoa now, shall we?"

Mrs. Ouma chuckled as the older woman took Mr. Ouma's arm. "Would you kids like to join us?" Mrs. Ouma asked. "We still owe you a cocoa from all the work this morning."

"Thanks—maybe later," Holly said before Ivy could speak up and accept. "We're supposed to meet our parents now."

"Yes, but thanks," Chris said. "And good throw, Mrs. K."

"Nice to meet you," Ivy added, smiling at the old woman. "Merry Christmas."

Holly led the way as the three kids hurried off, followed by Peppermint Bark. As soon as the adults were out of sight, the kids stopped.

"She seems nice," Ivy said, glancing back toward the dunking booth.

"She's great, but this is getting crazy," Holly said with a sigh. "Usually I love running into everyone in town at the festival. But maybe we should have looked around a little more before we came here. I mean, how are we supposed to search with everybody we know all over us?"

Chris shrugged. "We have to stay focused," he said. "Maybe next we should—"

"There you are!" a familiar voice cried out. *Very* familiar.

Holly smiled weakly and turned toward her parents, who were strolling toward the kids hand in hand. Dad wore the same clothes he'd had on that morning, but Mom had changed into nice slacks and a bright red coat.

Dad's eyes lighted up when he spotted Peppermint Bark—or rather, his leash and collar. "Aha!" Dad cried.

"I called your mother to ask her to bring my new tie and that belt, but she couldn't find either one."

"Yeah." Mom nudged him with her shoulder. "And your father accused me of having a blind spot when it comes to fashion. See? It wasn't my fault, Kenny!"

They both chuckled. Holly could tell they were in a good mood. And no wonder—it was Christmas! She sighed, for a second wishing she could forget about this whole quest and focus on having fun on her favorite holiday . . .

"Did you eat dinner yet, kids?" Dad smiled and patted his stomach. "Let's hit up Blitzen's Bar-B-Q—my treat. Ivy, you'll join us, right?"

"Thanks, Mr. Kerstman," Ivy said politely. "I am a little hungry."

Holly could see that Chris looked impatient. He tried to say that he wasn't hungry. But Mom and Dad were already heading toward the line of food trucks parked along the edge of the square. The kids had little choice but to follow.

"Thanks a lot, Ivy," Chris muttered. "Why'd you have to say you were hungry?"

"Drop it, Chris," Holly said, keeping her voice low so their parents wouldn't hear. "It's not like Mom and

Dad were going to let us skip—" She cut herself off with a gasp. "Hey, did you guys see that?"

"See what?" Chris was still glaring at Ivy.

"It was those elves!" Holly's heart pounded as she pointed into the crowd. "Right there—see? They're running toward the floats and stuff!"

"You sound like me, Hols," Ivy said with a smile. "Seeing elves everywhere."

"No, I'm serious!" Holly protested. "Didn't you see them?" She glanced at the others, but they all shook their heads, including Peppermint Bark.

"Sorry, Holly," the little dog barked. "It's so crowded, I can't see anything down here but lots of legs and shoes."

That made Chris and Ivy smile. But Holly was still peering toward the far end of the square, where the parade floats were waiting for their turn. And where she would have sworn she saw a pair of small figures with striped stocking caps and bright red tights . . .

"That was close!" Happy glanced over his shoulder as he followed Juniper through the space between two food trucks. "I think the taller girl saw us."

"I hope not," Juniper said grimly. "Now, hurry—we found a portal, thank goodness, so all we have to do is get Peppermint Bark and ourselves through it and safely back to the North Pole. But we need to find a way to nab him when those kids can't grab him back!"

Happy's long nose twitched as the scents of delicious Christmas treats from all over the world tickled it. "How are we going to do that?" he asked. "Maybe if we tried talking to them instead . . ."

"I already told you, we can't do that!" Juniper snapped. "Time is running out—we have to grab him and go! Besides, Mrs. Claus said—"

"I know, I know." Happy sighed. He still wasn't sure Mrs. Claus had meant that they couldn't say *anything* to *anyone*—especially if it meant getting Peppermint Bark home without all this running around. But it was hard to argue with Juniper.

"I heard the humans say something about a parade," Juniper said as she dashed out of the shadow of the food trucks and across a small parking lot. "Let's head that way and maybe something will—aha!" she interrupted herself, skidding to a stop.

This time, Happy managed to avoid crashing into her. "What is it, Juniper?" he asked.

Juniper pointed to a small bright-red vehicle parked in the lot. Happy had made a toy that looked just like it—only much smaller, of course—a few years earlier. "It's a moped," he said, proud to remember the name of the vehicle. "Humans use them to—"

"I know, I know. I've made toy ones too." Quick as a wink, Juniper hopped up onto the shiny leather seat and started fiddling with the controls. "Get up here, and let's see if we can figure out how to . . ."

Her next words were lost in the roar of the motor. With a squeak of surprise, Happy leaped up behind Juniper and held on to her waist as tightly as he could. He squeezed his eyes shut as a cloud of black exhaust surrounded the elves—but opened his eyes quickly when he felt the moped jerk into motion.

"Whee-e-e!" Juniper cried as the moped shot forward, barely missing a parked car. "Hey, this could actually be fun."

"What are you doing?" Happy shouted over the noise.

Juniper leaned forward over the handlebars, which her tiny arms could barely reach. She leaned to one side, which made the moped turn and speed out of the parking lot. "Rescuing Peppermint Bark, that's what!" she cried. "Now, hang on, and let's go!"

19

I Ruff a Parade

Chris had spent most of the past week wishing he could see more of his parents on Christmas Day, and now all he wished was that he could escape from them. They'd taken forever debating about what to order at the food trucks. Now everyone was sitting at a picnic table chowing down on their favorite festival food—spicy Indonesian stew for Chris, Jamaican curried goat for Mom, German Weisswurst for Ivy, Blitzen's burgers and barbecue for Dad and Holly. Dad had also ordered a rack of ribs with a side of mac and cheese for Peppermint Bark, who was eating under the table.

Chris finished his stew as quickly as he could. "All done!" he announced, wiping his face with a napkin. "May we be excused?"

Holly quickly shoved the rest of her fries into her mouth, along with the last bite of her burger. "Me too —I'm finished," she mumbled as she chewed.

"Settle down, kids." Dad was still working on his pulled pork sandwich. "It's Christmas! Sit back and soak it in."

"Hey." Ivy looked up. "Check it out—it's finally snowing!"

"Oh, it is!" Mom exclaimed, holding out her hand to catch a few flakes. "Look, Kenny—it's a white Christmas after all!"

She and Dad started humming "White Christmas" and swaying back and forth. Chris glanced at Holly and Ivy. How were they going to escape?

Suddenly Holly's eyes widened. "Heads up," she hissed. "Keep you-know-who under the table!"

Peppermint Bark poked his head out. "You mean me, right?" he barked.

"Shh!" Chris gently nudged him back. He'd just seen what his sister had seen—Mr. Brooks was striding straight toward them!

Oh no, Chris thought. *Did he hear that Peppermint Bark is here? Is he going to kick him out?*

But Mr. Brooks barely glanced at the kids. "Merry Christmas, Kerstmans," he said with a little bow. "Kenneth, I didn't get a chance to thank you for all your help earlier."

"It was my pleasure, Mr. Brooks." Dad smiled. "Thanks for organizing everything as always."

Mr. Brooks chuckled. "If I don't do it, who will?" he said. "In any case, we could use a couple more judges to ride on the head float and decide which homes and businesses win the prizes this year. Would you and your lovely wife like to step in?"

Dad traded a surprised look with Mom. Chris was a little surprised too. Usually the decoration judges were the most important people in town—the mayor, the head of the school board, people like that.

"Go for it, guys!" Holly said. "It sounds super fun."

"Well, I don't know," Mom said. "I was hoping we'd get to spend the rest of the evening as a family." She reached over and squeezed Chris's hand. "It's always hard being away from you kids on days like this."

Chris knew what she meant. And normally he would agree. But today—well, today wasn't exactly normal.

"I know, Mom," he said. "But we can hang out all day tomorrow, right? This is a big honor. You should do it."

"Yeah," Holly put in. "Go ahead—we'll clean up here." She gestured at the food wrappers and dirty napkins. "And we'll see you after the parade, right?"

Their parents still hesitated. But when Mr. Brooks cleared his throat, sounding a little impatient, Dad finally nodded. "It would be an honor," he said, climbing to his feet. He glanced around. "If you're really sure you kids don't mind . . ."

"Go!" Chris and Holly chorused, and Ivy nodded.

"Okay," Mom said, sounding a little wistful. "You kids are growing up so fast . . ." She got up and hurried around the table, grabbing Holly in a big hug.

Then it was Chris's turn. He wrapped his arms around his mother, breathing in the familiar scent of her shampoo. "Merry Christmas, Mom," he said.

"Merry Christmas, my beautiful, thoughtful boy." She hugged him hard. "I love you."

"Me too," Chris whispered, suddenly wanting to tell her everything—about who Peppermint Bark really was, their search for the portals, and the rest. But Mr. Brooks was watching, still looking impatient, and so Chris just hugged his mother once more and then let her go.

After more hugs all around from Dad, the adults disappeared into the crowd. Holly leaned down to look under the table.

"You can come out now," she told Peppermint Bark. "Time to get back to searching."

Chris was relieved to be able to return to their quest —but that feeling turned to panic when he checked the time. "It's almost ten o'clock!" he blurted out.

"Duh," his sister said. "The parade always starts at ten."

"No, I get it." Ivy glanced down at Peppermint Bark, who had crept out into view as soon as Mr. Brooks had disappeared. "We're really running out of time."

Chris looked at Peppermint Bark too. Barbecue sauce and melted cheese dotted the white fur around his mouth, which somehow made him look cuter than ever. Two hours. Would that be enough time to find another portal and get him home?

The girls were staring around the festival. "Where haven't we checked yet?" Holly said. "The Reindeer Raffle tent, the big tree . . ."

Ivy gasped. "I know! The parade!" she exclaimed.

"You mean the floats?" Holly nodded. "Good thinking. They're all super Christmasy. Let's go!"

She took off with Ivy at her heels. "Guess we're checking the floats next," Chris muttered, a little annoyed by how his sister still forgot he was around half the time.

Still, he had to admit she had a point. The parade would begin any moment now, winding its way all through town before returning to the square at midnight. If the kids wanted to look for a portal on the floats, it was now or never.

Chris blinked a snowflake out of his eye—the snow was coming down more steadily now, muffling the sounds of the festival and casting a pearly glow over the whole scene. "There are still more places to check," he told Peppermint Bark, trying to sound optimistic. "After the floats take off, we can check the big Christmas tree next—we haven't been over there yet."

He glanced toward the huge fir towering over the festival. A couple dozen people were gathered at the base, either looking at the ornaments or adding more of their own. Higher on the tree, strings of lights twinkled their way up to the giant silver star at the very top.

Chris blinked again, wondering if more snow was

getting in his eyes. Because something up near the star looked kind of blurry—almost like a swirling whirl-wind of snow . . .

"Hey, wait!" he blurted out.

But the girls were way ahead by then, almost lost in the crowd. Peppermint Bark was following them, but he paused and looked back.

"Are you coming, Chris?" he barked. "I can't wait to see the parade!"

Chris rushed after the others, his heart pounding. A portal—he'd just spotted a portal! He was sure of it!

He blinked more snow out of his eyes. Well, pretty sure, anyway . . .

When he caught up to the girls, they'd stopped at the edge of the staging area for the parade, which was at the border of the square near Noel Street. The place was packed with floats, bands, dancing groups, major-ettes, several people on horseback, and even eight bag-pipers wearing reindeer costumes.

Holly and Ivy were talking to three teenagers dressed in flowing robes who were standing beside a large flat-bed truck that had been turned into a live Nativity scene. Up on the float, someone reached up to switch on the bright electric star hanging from a frame. Chris rec-

ognized him right away, even in his Joseph costume—
it was Mr. Washington, his math teacher from last year.
Mary was there too—better known as Ms. Patel, who
worked in the same department as Chris's dad at PVU.
She had hitched up her blue and white robes and was
crouching down to soothe the real baby in the manger.
Several sheep were baaing in a little pen, and a rooster
and a couple of hens pecked at the sweet-smelling straw
scattered over the flatbed. Beside the float a large man
with a full beard led a bored-looking camel with one
hand and a sleepy donkey with the other. Chris recognized the man as the owner of a local petting zoo, who
went by the name of Lumberjack Lou.

"Check it out, Chris!" Holly waved him over. "Samantha is playing one of the wise men!"

"Wise people, she means." Chris and Holly's favorite
babysitter, who lived down the block from the Kerstmans, smiled at him. "Merry Christmas, guys."

"You too," Chris said automatically.

Two teenage boys were also dressed as wise people.
"I can't believe they want us to walk next to the float the
whole way," one of them grumbled. "There's plenty of
room up there!"

The second boy laughed. "Dude, maybe we should

take my new moped." He glanced toward the parking lot at the edge of the square. "I left it right over there. It'd be like a modern version of the Christmas story, right?"

"Dude! That would be awesome!" The first boy laughed, while Samantha rolled her eyes.

"You'd probably crash that thing," she said. "Especially now that it's snowing. I can't believe your parents actually got you a moped for Christmas."

The teenager noticed Chris looking at him. The older boy grinned. "It's a really awesome moped, little dude," he said. "Cherry red—perfect for this time of year, right? I'm not even sure my folks had anything to do with it. I think it came straight from Santa—he gave me the toy version when I was a kid, so he already knew I liked 'em! Wish I could thank that fat old dude."

Peppermint Bark's ears perked up. "You're welcome," he barked.

The teenager's eyes widened. "Yo, it's a dog!" he exclaimed. "Maybe he should be on the float too!"

Just then someone let out a loud whistle from the front of the line. "Heads up—we're starting," Samantha said. "Wish us luck!" She blew a kiss to the younger kids, then hurried over to take her place beside Lumberjack Lou, who was clucking to start the camel and donkey walking.

Soon the Nativity float was moving slowly, following the line of other floats, bands, and marchers toward the turn onto Noel Street. Chris tapped Holly on the arm. "Listen, I saw something," he said urgently.

Holly was squinting into the blowing snow, watching as another float rolled past—this one a winter wonderland theme, complete with ice skaters and giant papier-mâché penguins. The parade was picking up speed now as the first few floats moved up Noel Street. "Could that be a portal?" she said. "Oh wait—never mind. It's just silver confetti."

"That's the thing," Chris said. "I'm pretty sure I saw—hey!" he blurted out, interrupting himself as something swept past in a flash of red and the roar of a motor. Chris jumped back just in time to avoid being hit—and gasped as two small arms reached out and plucked Peppermint Bark right off the sidewalk! Before Chris could do more than gasp, the vehicle roared off, disappearing into the crowds milling around the departing floats.

"Stop!" Chris yelled. "They took him—they grabbed Peppermint Bark!"

Holly looked confused. "Who would grab him? Oh wait—maybe it was those guys. They said they wanted him on their float."

"Yeah, and that was a red moped like that kid was talking about," Ivy added. "Maybe they decided to come back for him."

Chris pushed his way through a throng of people snapping pictures of the floats, trying to follow the moped. But it was hard to make headway against the excited parade spectators. "We have to get him!" he cried.

Holly hauled him back by the hood of his coat. "Hang on—do we?" she said. "I mean, maybe this is a good thing. Like I said, they were probably just taking him up to the Nativity float. And if Peppermint Bark is part of the parade, it'll be easier for him to spot any portals he passes on the parade route."

"But there might not be one out there!" Chris exclaimed. He spun and pointed toward the Christmas tree, though it was hard to see clearly through the falling snow. "I saw one at the top of the tree!"

Ivy gasped. "Really? Are you sure?"

Chris hesitated. "Pretty sure," he said. "Anyway, it makes sense, right? Santa already hid one portal in a

Christmas tree—the one by the post office, remember?"

Without waiting for a response, he took off after the departing floats, sprinting out onto the street and running alongside the parade. A second later, Holly caught up.

"Okay, we'll try this your way," she said, pacing him easily. "But you'd better be right about that portal!"

Chris didn't answer. He just ran faster, dodging a local news crew shooting video, and almost skidding out on a patch of snow as he rounded the corner onto Noel. Within half a block he'd caught up to the winter wonderland float.

"Merry Christmas!" a woman dressed as a snow queen called to the spectators. "Let it snow!"

Chris winced as something bounced off his head— a small plastic-wrapped candy cane, one of a handful being tossed by the snow queen. Several young children raced over, shouting and shoving as they tried to grab the treats. People were pouring out of nearby houses, joining those who had followed the parade from the square, and it was getting more crowded all the time. The snow coated the streetlights, making it hard to see clearly.

"Look out!" Holly cried, cutting to one side just in time to avoid tripping over an excited little girl. "Coming through!"

Right in front of the winter wonderland float was a small marching band consisting mostly of middle-aged men with banjos. They were playing a twangy rendition of "Grandma Got Run Over by a Reindeer."

"Hey, watch it!" one of the men exclaimed as Chris slipped again on the snowy pavement and bumped into him.

"Sorry!" Chris called.

"Heads up!" Ivy caught up to him. "We need to detour."

Chris looked ahead and saw that they were almost at the bleachers set up near the town hall. The crowd was so thick there that he was sure it would take forever to shove their way through.

"Ugh," he muttered. The Nativity scene was just two floats ahead, but he could already see it passing the bleachers. Now what?

"This way!" Holly called, zooming sideways—right into the banjo band!

"Whoa, watch where you're going, young lady!" one of the band members exclaimed.

Chris thought the voice sounded like Mr. Berry from next door, though he didn't pause to confirm that. "Sorry, excuse us!" Chris called out, ducking his head and rushing after Holly. "Coming through!"

On the far side of the band, the way was a little clearer. "Hurry!" Holly panted as she, Chris, and Ivy turned and sprinted toward the front of the parade. "We're almost there!"

They passed an Old West–themed float flanked by a cowboy Santa on horseback. Fake antlers were attached to the horse's bridle. "Whoa, buckaroos!" Cowboy Santa called, while his horse snorted. "Where y'all off to in such an all-fired hurry?"

"Merry Christmas!" Chris called back as he sprinted past. The Nativity float was just ahead now . . .

But when they caught up to it, there was no sign of Peppermint Bark. Mary and Joseph waved calmly to the crowd, while the sheep munched the hay in their pen and let out an occasional *baa!* Samantha and the two boys were marching along on the far side with Lumberjack Lou and the larger animals.

"Come on," Holly said, falling back just long enough to dash across the street behind the float.

Samantha looked surprised when she saw them. "What are you doing here?" she asked.

"The dog," Chris panted, so out of breath that he could hardly get the words out. "Peppermint Bark. Where is he?"

The teenagers all looked confused. "You mean that little white dog?" the moped guy said. "I thought he was with you."

"You didn't grab him?" Holly sounded less out of breath than Chris. He figured all those years of playing soccer and running track had paid off for her. "But we thought we saw your moped . . ."

"Grab the dog?" Samantha looked more perplexed than ever. "Of course not!"

"My moped?" The teenager looked alarmed now. "Dudes, I told you I thought I saw it speed by! What if it got, like, moped-jacked?"

"You saw it?" Chris panted. "Where'd it go?"

The kid pointed straight ahead. "That way!"

The other teenage boy nodded. "We figured it was, like, a police moped taking a VIP up to the judges' float or something."

"We've got to catch up," Chris said, gasping for breath.

"You guys look beat," Holly said, glancing from Chris to Ivy, who also looked tired. "I can try to run ahead and look for him while you walk and rest if you want."

Chris shook his head, too out of breath to respond. He couldn't give up now. What if his sister let him down, the way she had so often lately? Still, he wasn't sure he'd ever be able to run fast enough to catch up to that moped . . .

Just then the camel let out a loud snort and stopped. *Plop!* A large pile of manure landed in the snow, steaming in the cold night air.

"Oh man," Lumberjack Lou muttered. "Better clean that up . . ."

He switched both lead ropes to one hand, then reached up to grab a bag out of the pack on his back. Chris blinked as a crazy idea popped into his head.

"Here, let me hold that for you," he said, grabbing the donkey's lead out of the bearded man's hand. Quick as a wink, Chris vaulted up onto the creature's back and gave him a stout kick with both heels. "Giddyup!" Chris yelled.

With a loud bray of alarm, the donkey flattened his ears and took off at a gallop.

20

Fa-La-La Hee Haw

"Whoa!" Chris cried, scrabbling to cling to the donkey's tufty mane. "I didn't mean you had to go quite this fast . . ."

Chris glanced over his shoulder. Lumberjack Lou was shaking his fist, trying to hold on to the suddenly prancing camel. Just then the donkey veered to the left, and Chris turned forward again, totally focused on not falling off.

The donkey let out another loud bray, then stampeded into a group of Mexican folk dancers dressed in bright holiday costumes. *"Cuidado!"* one of the dancers yelled. "Look out, everyone!"

"Sorry!" Chris yelled back, hanging on for dear life as the donkey burst out the far side of the group. "Please, donkey—turn back and follow the parade! I have to get to Peppermint Bark!"

Suddenly there was a faint bark from somewhere up ahead. It was Peppermint Bark!

"I'm coming, buddy!" Chris yelled. Just then the donkey leaped over a curb, and Chris gritted his teeth and wrapped his arms around the creature's neck to keep from bouncing off. "At least, I'm trying . . ."

There was more barking. Chris tried to hear what Peppermint Bark was saying, but couldn't make out the words over the noise of the parade and the moped motor and the donkey's galloping hoofbeats—not to mention the pounding of Chris's own heart.

Then Chris realized the donkey had slowed his breakneck pace, at least slightly. His large ears were pitched toward the sound of the barks. He seemed to be listening . . .

Suddenly he let out a bray so loud that it rattled Chris's eardrums. A second later Peppermint Bark barked again, and this time Chris heard his words: "Hey, Chris, Paco says he'll help us!" the little dog was calling. "Hold on tight!"

"Paco," Chris said, smiling as he realized that must be the donkey's name—and that the donkey had just spoken to Peppermint Bark. "I guess you've got the Christmas spirit too!"

Then Chris stopped talking, since the donkey had turned to canter alongside the parade. Within seconds they'd caught up to the moped, which was stuck in the midst of some enthusiastic flag twirlers and cheerleaders wearing the red and green colors of Poinsettia High School.

"One, two, three, four, who's the guy we're rooting for?" one of the cheerleaders cried.

"Santa! Santa! Santa!" the rest of the group chanted.

Paco slowed to a walk to keep pace. Chris squinted through the high schoolers, but it was hard to catch more than a glimpse of the moped through all the movement. Still, he was pretty sure he could see Peppermint Bark's white fur.

"Okay, Paco," Chris told the donkey. "We're going in . . ."

Paco snorted loudly, then turned—and charged straight into the pep squad! The girls squealed in alarm and leaped aside, doing backflips and cartwheels to get out of the way. Chris winced, hoping nobody got hurt. But the donkey was more sure-footed than Chris expected, dodging the slower girls and leaping over a dropped baton.

"Peppermint Bark!" Chris blurted out as they reached the moped. The donkey barely slowed down as they swept past—and the little white dog leaped up into Chris's arms!

"Chris! You came!" Peppermint Bark exclaimed. "I tried to tell those guys I needed to say goodbye before we head back to—"

"Never mind that," Chris interrupted. "Can you tell this donkey to go back to the square? Because I saw a portal!"

"You did?" Peppermint Bark cried. "Then let's go!"

Soon they were galloping back into Poinsettia Square. It was getting late, and many festival-goers had left, either to watch the parade or to go home to bed. Still, the place was crowded enough that Paco's arrival didn't go unnoticed. From every direction came shouts of "Runaway donkey!" and "Heads up!"

Chris held on tightly as Paco skidded to a stop at the base of the huge town Christmas tree, leaving tracks in the snow. "Thanks, Paco!" Peppermint Bark barked as he and Chris jumped down, trying to ignore the startled stares of several people who were hanging ornaments nearby.

The donkey brayed, and Chris almost thought he understood what Paco was saying: *You're welcome, and merry Christmas!*

Chris gave Paco a pat, then gestured to Peppermint Bark. "Come on, we have to get up to the top," Chris called. "I'll climb and carry you."

"Okay, Chris," Peppermint Bark said. "But maybe we should wait for—"

"No time—we don't want this one to close too." Chris glanced around, realizing that Peppermint Bark was right—Holly and Ivy should be here for this. For one thing, Chris was still tired from all the running, and donkey riding wasn't as easy as it looked. It would have been nice to have some help getting Peppermint Bark to the top of the tree . . .

But the girls were nowhere in sight, and there was no time to wait for them. Not this close to midnight, with the portal ready to close at any time. It was all up to Chris. Tired or not, he would just have to do his best . . .

Peppermint Bark sniffed the air. "You guys are right, Chris!" he barked. "I can smell it now—there's definitely a portal up there!"

Chris wasn't sure what Peppermint Bark meant by "you guys," since Holly and Ivy hadn't even seen the portal. But that didn't matter right now. "I know," Chris said. "Now, let's get you home!"

He raced toward the tree, already looking for the best branch to start climbing. There were several people hanging ornaments on the other side of the tree, but nobody on this side at the moment. He was only steps away when a tall, lean figure stepped out to block his path.

"Stop right there, young man!" Mr. Brooks commanded.

Chris skidded to a stop just in time to avoid crashing into the man. He goggled up at him. "Wh-what are you doing here?" Chris blurted out. "I thought . . ."

His mind flashed to the judges' float. Why wasn't Mr. Brooks on it?

But it didn't really matter. He was here now, and he didn't look happy.

"I thought I told you to keep a leash on that dog," Mr. Brooks said, glaring at Peppermint Bark.

Chris gulped. Dad's candy cane tie still dangled around the little dog's neck, but he seemed to have lost the Santa-print belt during his wild parade experience.

"Um . . ." Chris began, shooting a worried look toward the top of the tree. It was still snowing, and he couldn't really see the portal at all. But Peppermint Bark had just smelled it, so Chris knew it was still there —if only they could reach it before it was too late . . .

"Well?" Mr. Brooks demanded, crossing his arms over his chest. "What do you have to say for yourself, Christopher? Shall we go find your parents and discuss this rebellious behavior with them, hmm?"

For a split second, Chris was ready to give up. He was exhausted, and nobody disobeyed Mr. Brooks—not even the mayor. What had Chris been thinking, anyway? He wasn't a rebel, or an action star, or a superhero . . .

But then he glanced down at Peppermint Bark. Santa's puppy gazed up at him, his brown eyes worried but trusting. Chris knew he couldn't let his friend down.

"Here's what I have to say," he told Mr. Brooks, quickly unzipping his parka about halfway. "Pardon me —coming through!"

Chris swooped down, grabbed Peppermint Bark,

and dashed past the sputtering Mr. Brooks. "Stop right there!" the man cried.

Chris ignored him. "Hold on," he told Peppermint Bark, shoving the little dog into the front of his parka and zipping it shut. Then, before Mr. Brooks could catch up, Chris grabbed a prickly fir branch and started to climb.

21

O Christmas Tree

Happy ran as fast as he could, but even so, it was hard to keep up with Juniper. They'd ditched the moped at the entrance to the town square, and now they were running toward the beautiful big Christmas tree at the center.

"There he is!" Juniper cried, pointing. "The naughty boy is climbing the tree with him!"

"Oh!" Happy panted. "Maybe he's not naughty after all. Maybe he's taking Peppermint Bark to the portal!"

Juniper slowed down just long enough to turn her head and glare at him. "What would a human child know about portals?" she snapped. "But hurry—it could close at any moment, just like the others. If I get trapped in this ridiculous place for the entire year, I'll never forgive that pup . . ."

Still muttering under her breath, she ran to the tree and started climbing. Happy followed, shooting a curious glance toward a skinny older man who was shaking his fist up at the festively decorated tree.

"Be happy," the elf called down to the man. "It's Christmas!"

Then Happy focused on his climbing, trying to keep up with Juniper. She was moving fast, dodging Christmas ornaments of all shapes and sizes, from huge glass balls to handmade craft-stick snowflakes. Happy wished he had time to stop and admire them all.

I don't think being stuck here would be all bad, he thought, glancing out at the town, with its twinkling lights everywhere and beautiful snow just beginning to coat the roads and rooftops. *It's almost as nice as the North Pole.*

"Happy!" the other elf shouted. "Keep up!"

"Coming, Juniper." Happy grabbed the next branch, following her upward.

They caught up to the boy and dog a few yards below the portal. The boy was breathing hard as he hauled himself steadily from one branch to the next.

"Don't look down, Chris," Peppermint Bark barked. "We're almost there!"

"Stop!" Juniper shouted. "Give me that puppy!"

The boy flinched, so startled that he almost lost his grip on the branch. "Who's there?" he cried, peering down.

"It's okay!" Happy called from his spot just behind Juniper. "We're here to help. We just have to—"

Juniper didn't give him time to finish. "We're taking the dog!" she snapped. Quick as a wink, she scrambled up and past the boy, grabbing Peppermint Bark as she went.

"Hey!" the boy cried. "Wait!"

He lurched upward, trying to grab the little dog back. Happy gasped as he saw the boy's foot slip on the snow-slick branch . . .

"Aaaah!" Chris cried, grabbing for another branch and missing. Even as he felt himself falling backwards, he saw the small woman—an elf?—and Peppermint Bark leaping upward toward the portal.

"I've got you!" Suddenly strong hands grabbed Chris by the collar of his parka. Tiny hands. Chris found himself dangling high above Poinsettia Square, held only by a smiling little person clinging to the tree by his pointy-toed boots.

"You're . . . you're an elf," Chris blurted out. "Like, a *real* one!"

"That's right—Happy's my name, and toy making's my game." The elf hauled Chris up until the boy could grab a sturdy branch.

"Thanks," Chris said, already looking up. He gasped when he saw that the other elf had carried Peppermint Bark almost all the way up to the portal.

"Don't fret," Happy said. "Juniper's taking Peppermint Bark home again." He glanced upward and lowered his voice to a soft squeak. "I'm not supposed to tell you that, but it's true."

"I know," Chris said. "I mean, I see that now." Suddenly all those weird elf sightings made sense—in the bushes outside the post office, at Jingle Junction, and riding that moped through the parade. Of course someone at the North Pole had missed Peppermint Bark!

Of course they weren't planning to leave him here for a whole year!

But there was no time to think about that. Chris grabbed a higher branch, trying to haul himself up with arms that suddenly felt like overcooked spaghetti noodles.

"Wait!" he cried. "I just want to say goodbye . . ."

Happy gasped. "Oh, of course you do!" he exclaimed. "Hang on—I'll take you."

The elf leaped upward, grabbing Chris as he went by. He jumped from branch to branch, heading for the portal. Chris's head spun as he found himself upside down, bumping against scratchy fir boughs and briefly catching a foot in the light cord before shaking it loose . . . Would they get there in time?

"Juniper, wait!" Happy cried in his high, squeaky voice.

But the other elf didn't pause or look back. She was at the portal now. Holding Peppermint Bark tightly with both arms, she leaped right into the swirling vortex . . .

SLURP!

Both elf and dog disappeared! Chris gasped. "No-o-o-o!" he cried.

"Juniper!" Happy shouted, still moving upward, faster now than ever.

Suddenly Chris felt something—like a force field grabbing him, pulling him upward along with the little elf. The portal loomed right in front of them; snow and twinkling lights were swirling, swirling . . . Chris was enveloped by the strong scents of gingerbread and pinecones, and Christmas music filled the air . . .

22

Portal Panic

"There he is!" Holly shouted, pointing. "I can't believe it —he's climbing the Christmas tree!"

Ivy caught up, panting hard. "Oh my gosh," she said breathlessly, peering ahead through the falling snow. "He is!"

Holly just stood there for a second, staring up at her brother. He looked really small way up there, more than halfway up the huge tree. When she glanced toward the top of the tree, she gasped.

"He was right—there's a portal!" she exclaimed, blinking away a snowflake that had landed on her eyelashes. Then she frowned. "Wait—am I seeing things, or are there some other people up there?"

"Where?" Ivy wiped her eyes with her glove. "I can't see anything through all this snow!"

"Never mind—come on. We have to get him." Holly raced toward the tree, not taking her eyes off her brother. "I mean, he's getting really close to that—"

She cut herself off with another gasp and stopped. Chris had just disappeared!

"Oh no!" she yelled. "I think he fell into the portal!"

"What?" Ivy looked horrified. "But . . ."

Holly was already running again. She had to save her brother!

But more than a dozen people were milling around at the base of the tree. Some were hanging ornaments, others were watching the snow, and a woman was petting the donkey, who was now calmly nibbling the lower branches. Holly spotted her soccer coach in the crowd, along with the Oumas, Mrs. Kasabian, and a few other friends and neighbors.

Then Holly noticed one more familiar face. A very annoyed-looking Mr. Brooks was stomping toward her.

"Stop, Holly Kerstman!" he cried, pointing a

knobby-knuckled finger at her. "Do you know what your brother just did?"

"Uh-huh." Holly craned her neck to look upward. "That's why I'm here, okay?"

She tried to dodge past, but Mr. Brooks grabbed her by the shoulder. His fingers felt like a crab's pincers digging in through her coat and scarf.

"I said stop," he warned.

The other people near the tree had noticed the commotion by then. Mrs. Kasabian hobbled closer with her walker.

"What's all the hubbub?" she asked. "The kids are just here to add their ornaments, yes?"

"No," Mr. Brooks growled.

"Um . . ." Ivy said uncertainly.

But Holly had just seen her opportunity. "Yes!" she cried. "That's exactly why we're here!"

"I knew it." Mrs. Kasabian nodded and smiled at Holly. "It's so nice to see young people with true Christmas spirit!"

"That's not why they're here at all," Mr. Brooks snapped. "Do you see any ornaments in their hands?"

By now, Ivy had caught on to Holly's plan. "Here's mine!" She quickly unwrapped the ivy-embroidered scarf from around her neck. "I thought this would make a beautiful garland."

As she hung it on the tree, Mrs. Kasabian and the other onlookers oohed and aahed. Mr. Brooks looked more annoyed than ever.

"And you?" he asked, quirking an eyebrow at Holly.

Holly reached for her own scarf, then realized she must have lost it somewhere along the way. What could she use instead?

Oh no, she thought frantically. *I don't have anything that will work as an ornament!* Then, suddenly, she gulped, remembering something. *Or do I . . . ?*

Slowly, she reached up and pulled the birthstone necklace out from beneath her coat. Ivy gasped when she saw it.

"Oh, Holly, no," Ivy whispered.

Holly hesitated, running her fingers over the smooth surface of the gemstone. Then she looked up toward the spot where her little brother had disappeared . . .

"Here," she said, pulling off the necklace and holding it out. "This is what I want to hang on the tree." She swallowed hard. "It's . . . it's very special. But I have to do it."

"Lovely, Holly," Mrs. Kasabian said with a smile. "Let her through, Mr. Brooks."

Mr. Brooks gnashed his teeth, for a moment looking as if he wouldn't let Holly through. But finally he stepped aside.

"Fine," he said. "Hang your so-called ornaments. I'll still be here when you've finished."

"Whatever." Holly walked forward and looped the necklace over a branch.

Beside her, Ivy looked up. "Um, shouldn't we hang them a little higher, Hols?" she prompted.

Holly gulped, realizing Ivy expected her to lead the way in climbing the tree. Climbing the tall, tall tree . . .

Her hands shaking, Holly reached for a branch and pulled herself up. But she slipped off, landing with a grunt.

"Are you okay?" Ivy asked.

"No!" Holly hissed, her face going red. "No, I'm not, okay? I'm . . . I'm afraid of heights!"

Ivy blinked. "You're what?" she said uncertainly. "Um, is this a joke or something? Like, are you making fun of me for the dog thing earlier?"

"No!" Holly clenched her fists inside her gloves. "I've always been afraid! Why do you think I had to go to the nurse with a stomachache the day we climbed ropes in gym?"

"Oh." Ivy blinked again and nodded. "Yeah, that did seem strange—especially since you never get stomachaches." She grabbed Holly's hand and squeezed it. "But listen, you can do anything, Hols! I know it's scary to face your fears and stuff, and I'm not saying it's easy. But if I could pick up a dog—and even become friends with one!—then you can do this. I know you can!"

Just then came an angry shout from across the square. Holly glanced over her shoulder and saw Lumberjack Lou racing toward them. The camel was nowhere in sight, but the donkey pricked his long ears at his owner.

"Uh-oh," Ivy whispered. "That donkey guy looks pretty mad . . ."

"Yeah." Holly swallowed hard and looked up. "Maybe you're right, Ives. If you really think I can do this . . ."

"I know you can!" Ivy smiled at her. "Besides, Chris needs you, right?"

"Right." With one last deep breath, Holly grabbed the branch again. And this time, she held on tightly, pulling herself up until she could wedge her feet onto a stout branch a few feet off the ground.

"Don't look down," Ivy said. "Come on—you can follow me."

Ivy swung herself up to another branch. Holly reached up to follow her when someone grabbed her leg.

"Hey!" she blurted out, looking down. It was Lumberjack Lou!

"Get down here, little girl," he growled. "You and your brother have some explaining to do . . ."

Holly tried to shake her leg loose. But Lou's grip was like iron.

"Let her go!" Ivy yelled.

"Yeah! We have to find Chris!" Holly added.

But she already knew it was no use. It was all over —they'd failed. Now what would happen to her little brother?

"Hey!" Suddenly Mr. and Mrs. Ouma appeared beside Lumberjack Lou. "Let her go, sir," Mr. Ouma ordered sternly.

Lou glanced at him. "Why should I? They stole my donkey!"

"Isn't that your donkey right over there?" Mrs. Ouma pointed at the donkey, who was standing there with a few sprigs of fir sticking out of his mouth, chewing thoughtfully.

"Well, yeah, but . . . uh . . ." Lou sputtered.

Mr. Ouma crossed his arms over his chest. "These are good kids," he told Lou. "The kind of kids anyone would be proud to have as neighbors."

"That's right. If they were donkey thieves, they'd admit it. So let her go!" Mrs. Ouma poked Lou in the chest, startling him—and causing him to loosen his grip on Holly's leg.

She didn't hesitate, kicking free and then swinging up to the higher branch beside Ivy—too high for Lou to reach from the ground.

"Don't stop!" Ivy cried, already scrambling for the next branch. "He might try to climb after us."

Holly nodded and followed her friend. But she couldn't resist one last glance down at the Oumas. They'd lived across the street forever, but Holly didn't know them that well. And after what had happened to their holiday display today, she wouldn't have guessed they'd stick up for her the way they just had.

Ivy looked down too. "Thanks, Mr. and Mrs. Ouma!" she called, waving at the couple before continuing her climb.

Holly's eyes widened as she realized what had happened. This was all because Ivy had insisted on helping to clean up the mess Peppermint Bark had made earlier! *Wow*, Holly thought. *Who knew a little thing like that could make such a difference?*

But there wasn't time to ponder it just then. The snow was coming down harder now, making the branches and needles of the tree slippery. Holly needed to focus on her climbing.

"This is crazy," she panted as she pulled herself from one branch to the next, not daring to look down anymore. The voices from below had faded, and all she could see were the snowy branches around her and Ivy's boots just above. "We're never going to make it all the way up there!"

"I can see it!" Ivy called, sounding excited. "The portal—we're getting close!" Then she gasped loudly. "But wait—I think it's getting smaller!"

"What?" Holly yanked herself upward.

Now she could see it too—the portal! But her friend was right. Even as Holly watched, she could see it shrinking. Closing. With her little brother inside!

Oh no! Holly thought, as she imagined an entire year without Chris around. Sure, he could be annoying sometimes. But he was her brother, and her heart broke when she tried to imagine life without him . . .

23

The North Pole

Chris wasn't sure how long the trip through the portal lasted. A long time? A few seconds? He was so dizzy and discombobulated that there was no way to tell.

But finally he felt himself launched into the air . . .

"OOF!" he grunted as he landed on a pillowy pile of snow.

A second later, the portal spit Happy out beside him.

As Chris sat up, his head spinning, he saw the other elf, the one Happy had called Juniper, digging her way out of a snow pile nearby. And then another figure burst out of the same snow pile. Peppermint Bark!

"We made it! Hooray!" the little dog cried, shaking the snow from his fur. Then he blinked. "Hey, Chris, you're here too! Wow! Welcome to the North Pole!"

Chris's eyes widened. Were they really at the North Pole? He looked around. The four of them were on a vast, desolate, snow-swept plain. A short distance away, huge peppermint-striped gates rose out of the snow, wide open. Beyond the gates he could glimpse the spires of a white snow castle . . .

Juniper was on her feet by now, brushing the snow from her tunic. She pointed at Chris. "Who brought the human along? Oh, never mind—we have to get inside the gates! Now!"

"Wait." Chris was feeling confused. "But I . . ."

Then there was a loud burping sound from nearby. Two more people came flying out of the portal and landed in the snow. Holly and Ivy!

"Chris!" Holly cried, spitting out a mouthful of snow as she jumped to her feet. "You're okay!" She raced forward and grabbed him in a hug so tight he couldn't breathe for a second.

Then she shoved him away so hard he staggered back and almost fell. She glared at him.

"You almost gave me a heart attack, you know," she

snapped. "When I saw you disappear through the portal . . ."

"Never mind all that!" Juniper was dancing frantically, waving her tiny arms. "We really need to get inside before the gates close!"

Peppermint Bark gasped. "You're right," he said. "Look—they're starting to shut now!"

Everyone spun to look. Sure enough, the enormous gates were creaking slowly toward each other.

"Run!" Happy hollered.

The whole group raced toward the gates. Peppermint Bark was in the lead, though the elves weren't far behind. Next came Holly, pumping her arms the way she did in the sprints at track meets.

"Come on," Chris yelled to Ivy, who was bringing up the rear. When he glanced back to check on her, his foot hit a patch of ice, sending him flying forward.

"Oof!" he said as he felt cold snow go down his collar and into his shoes.

"Are you okay?" Ivy shouted. "Get up—hurry!"

Chris stood and tried to run, but his foot skidded again on the ice and he let out a shout as his ankle twisted painfully. When he tried to get up again, that leg collapsed under him, dumping him back in the snow. Meanwhile the gates were still swinging shut . . .

"Go ahead without me!" he yelled, knowing there was no way he could make it in time. But everyone else still could . . .

"Chris!" Holly turned and ran back toward him. "Come on, get up—I'll help you," she said, grabbing him by the arm and trying to yank him to his feet.

Ivy had stopped beside Chris and tried to help too. "Hurry, hurry!" she cried, looking terrified.

Happy the elf came rushing back. "Happy, stop!" Juniper yelled.

"We can't abandon him!" Happy exclaimed. "What kind of Christmas spirit would that be?"

Juniper blinked. "Oh. Maybe you're right." She turned and ran back toward Chris too.

Peppermint Bark was so far ahead he hadn't heard Chris go down. He reached the gates and paused, looking back for the others. Where were they?

He peered through the falling snow, finally spotting

them far behind him—almost all the way back at the portal.

"Hurry, hurry!" he barked. "It's almost time!"

"Chris fell!" Holly called, her words so far away that even Peppermint Bark's sharp ears barely caught them. "You should keep going, though—you made it! We got you home, just like we promised!"

Peppermint Bark glanced through the gates. The castle was there, gleaming white and welcoming. He could picture his cozy spot at the foot of Santa's comfy chair in front of the fireplace . . .

I'll miss that, he thought. *But it's only for a year. Santa will understand. Chris needs me!*

"I'm coming!" the little dog cried, bounding through the snow. "I'm coming—I won't leave you!"

By the time Peppermint Bark reached the others, Chris was back on his feet hobbling along between Holly and Ivy. The elves were dancing around, urging them forward.

"Hurry!" Juniper cried. "Maybe we'll still be able to—"

CLANG!

24

Ho Ho Ho Uh-Oh . . .

Chris felt his heart stop when the great gates clanged shut. But then it started up again, beating faster than ever. "Oh no," he said. "Now what?"

Juniper crossed her arms and glared at him. "Now we're stuck, that's what!" she exclaimed. "If only you meddling humans had left it to us, Peppermint Bark would be home and none of us would be out here!"

Holly rolled her eyes. "Leave him alone, okay?" she said. "It's not like you guys told us you were there to help Peppermint Bark."

Chris glanced at her, realizing his sister must have

worked out why the elves had gone to Poinsettia. That wasn't a surprise—Holly was smart like that.

"Okay," he said. "Can we go back through the . . ." His words faded away as he glanced toward the portal. Or, rather, the spot where the portal had been. There was no sign of it now.

Happy followed his gaze. "The portals won't open until next Christmas," he said. "Just like the gates."

They all turned to stare at the gates. Peppermint Bark wagged his tail weakly. "Look on the bright side," he barked. "I heard some wolves live out here—maybe we can find an abandoned wolf den to live in for the year . . ."

Happy groaned, and Juniper muttered under her breath. Chris could tell the little dog was trying to stay cheerful, but there didn't seem to be much point.

"Wolves?" Holly exclaimed. "Great, just great!" She whirled toward Chris. "I can't believe this is happening!"

"I'm sorry!" Peppermint Bark cried. "This is all my fault—I asked you to help!"

"Don't bother—she'd much rather blame me!" Suddenly Chris was just as fed up with Holly as she obviously was with him. "She blames me for everything!"

"What? That's not what I meant at all! Anyway, no,

I don't—*you're* the one who's always getting *me* in trouble," Holly said.

"Guys . . ." Ivy began.

But Chris barely heard her. "How do you think it feels when you act like this?" he asked his sister. "Like I'm some . . . some baby who can't do anything right. Like you'd rather I wasn't even around."

"What?" Holly cried. "If I don't want you around, why'd I climb up that tree and jump through the portal to save you?"

Chris crossed his arms and turned away. "I don't know," he said. "But it's like I don't even know you anymore. Like I'm all alone, left out of my own sister's life."

"See?" Juniper said to Happy sharply. "This is what happens when you get involved with humans."

"It's not my fault," Happy protested. "I wanted to tell them what we were doing all along!"

Chris glanced at Ivy, waiting for her to start yelling too. But she was staring down at the snow, being very quiet.

"Ho ho ho!" Suddenly a cheerful voice rang out from the direction of the snow castle.

Peppermint Bark gasped. "Santa?"

Chris spun around just in time to see an enormous

sleigh, pulled by eight large reindeer, fly over the gates. Holding the reins was a jolly man with a white beard, a red suit, and a smile merry and bright enough to light up the entire world.

"Santa!" Happy and Juniper cried, running toward the gates.

The sleigh swooped down, landing right in front of the group. "I heard we had some visitors out here," Santa said with a wink. He snapped his fingers, and the huge gates behind him started creaking open again. "Welcome! Please come right in . . ."

Chris and the others didn't have to be invited twice. And it wasn't until they were inside that Chris realized his ankle felt as good as new, even though he'd been pretty sure it was sprained . . .

But there was no time to wonder about that. As soon as Santa stepped down from his sleigh, Peppermint Bark leaped into his arms. "I'm sorry I stowed away!" the little dog cried, licking Santa's nose. "This is all my fault!"

Santa hugged him and chuckled. "Never mind, little buddy," he said. "No harm done, eh?"

"But the gates . . ." Juniper was staring at the open gates, looking confused.

Santa chuckled again. "Ah, that part's my fault," he said, laying a finger aside of his nose and winking. "You see, I tried out some new tech this year—SPS."

"SPS?" Holly echoed. "What's that?"

"Santa Positioning System." Santa let out another *ho ho ho*. "Mrs. Claus just invented it this year, and like most of her inventions, it works like a charm. It helped me find my way around the world so quickly that I finished early! So when I got back here, I closed the gates myself—didn't see any reason to keep them open, at least not until I heard about Peppermint Bark going missing. In any case, they won't lock for another hour. So come on inside—Mrs. Claus will have hot cocoa for everyone!"

The next forty-five minutes passed like a dream. Chris could hardly believe he was here—at the North Pole, touring Santa's castle, meeting Mrs. Claus and the reindeer and the rest of the elves . . . It was magical! Peppermint Bark led them around the entire place, offering them delicious Christmas cookies in the cozy kitchen, showing them his favorite napping spots and the view of the skating pond from the east tower . . . There was so much to see!

"And we've saved the best for last," Happy announced when they came back into the grand front hall after touring the reindeer stable.

Mrs. Claus kicked off her snow boots and chuckled. She didn't look or act quite how Chris had expected—for instance, he definitely hadn't expected her to start swapping ski stories with Ivy, who had been on several ski trips in Japan, or to demonstrate her unique design for the huge central fireplace that burned eco-friendly pellets. But she was just as jolly and kind as Santa himself . . . so come to think of it, maybe she was *exactly* like Chris had expected.

"Best for last? Let me guess," Mrs. Claus said, winking at Happy. "The workshop?"

Ivy gasped. "You mean the elves' workshop?" she exclaimed.

"Of course!" Peppermint Bark said with a laugh. "Where do you think all those toys come from? Let's go!"

He led the way down a short set of stone steps. Happy threw open a pair of wooden doors. "Here's where the magic happens!" he cried.

A couple dozen elves were inside, including Juniper. All of them were singing together—"Carol of the Bells" in three-part harmony. Chris stared in amazement at the little worktables, the tools, and the stacks of wood and other material. "This is amazing!" he said.

Holly and Ivy looked as overwhelmed as he felt. "Wow," Ivy said. "It's just like I always imagined!"

Holly shrugged. "But who knew elves were such great singers?"

"Thanks!" Happy exclaimed. "Come on, guys— let's do another one!"

Juniper took a deep breath. *"Dashing through the snow in a one-horse open sleigh . . ."* she began.

Ivy sang along for a few lines. Then she stopped and looked over at Santa. "So wait—I've always wondered about the others?"

"The others?" Santa raised both shaggy white eyebrows.

Ivy nodded. "You know—fairies, mermaids, the Easter Bunny . . . Do you know them? Are they all real —even mermaids?"

Santa chuckled. "Oh, *those* others!" He winked. "I'll never tell!"

Chris smiled, feeling happier than he had in a long time. Somehow, there inside the cozy walls of the snow castle, he could feel things thawing between himself and his sister. Did she feel it too?

He sneaked a peek over at her. Holly was looking back at him. She smiled uncertainly.

"Um, sorry," she said. "You know—about the stuff we said earlier? I really do like having you around, even if I don't always show it."

"Really?" Chris held his breath, hardly daring to believe it.

Holly rolled her eyes. "Of course, really, you dork!" she exclaimed. Then she grabbed him in a big hug. "We're family, okay? And I wouldn't trade you for anyone."

Ivy sighed, watching them. Chris glanced at her. "What's wrong?" he asked, realizing he actually wanted to know—to make sure she was okay. Because after all they'd just been through, Ivy didn't seem so much like his sister's annoying friend anymore. At least not *only* that. She seemed like his friend, too.

Ivy sighed again. "You guys are so lucky. I've always wanted a brother or sister . . ." She touched her birthstone necklace. "That's why I wanted you to have a necklace like mine, Hols. I thought it would make us seem more like sisters." She smiled shyly at Chris. "Like I was part of your family."

Peppermint Bark wagged his tail. "I know what you mean," he barked. "I know how it feels to be all alone."

Chris bent down to rub the little dog's ears. "I know. I'm glad you're home." He realized he meant it, too. Sure, he'd miss Peppermint Bark like crazy when he and Holly and Ivy went home. But this was where Santa's puppy belonged—with Santa, doing his job, helping bring Christmas to everyone in the world.

Peppermint Bark licked the boy's hand. "Thanks, Chris," he said. "I probably never would have made it if not for you and Holly and Ivy."

Juniper heard him and stopped singing. "Hey, what about me?" she said. Then she glanced over at Happy. "Uh, I mean, *us.* Happy and I would've rescued you even earlier if they hadn't gotten in the way." She stared at the kids.

Peppermint Bark laughed. "Maybe," he said. "On the other hand, these guys would have done it without you, too. Holly never stopped trying to think of a plan. Ivy knows everything about magic and stuff like that, and she's super brave." He wagged his tail and looked up at Chris. "And Chris? Well, he never stopped believing in the Christmas spirit—or in me. He's a great friend."

"Thanks. So are you." Chris dropped to his knees and hugged Peppermint Bark tightly.

Santa beamed as he watched them. "Friends and family are the greatest gift of all—at Christmas or any other time of the year," he said. Then he snapped his fingers. "Ah, and speaking of gifts . . ."

He dug into the pocket of his red coat. When he took his hand out, something sparkly and gold dangled from his fingers.

Holly gasped. "My necklace!" she cried.

Santa handed it to her. "It was very generous, what you did," he said solemnly. "You sacrificed something you wanted very, very much to save your brother. That puts you on my good list for sure."

"Thanks, Santa." Holly clutched the necklace, looking happy. She glanced over at Chris. "You're right, I love this necklace. But I'd do exactly the same thing all over again if I had to. Friends and family are more important than things."

"I totally agree." Ivy touched her own necklace again, smiling first at Holly and then at Chris.

Chris smiled back, not sure what to say. But he knew one thing: this was the best Christmas ever!

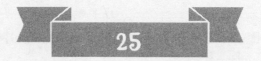

25

Merry and Bright

Chris had just finished his third cup of cocoa when Santa stood up. "Sorry to cut this short, everyone," Santa's voice boomed. "But it's time to go. Soon the gates will close for real—and the last of the portals with them. I need to get you kids home, or your parents will never forgive me."

As he chuckled, Happy and Juniper traded a look. "Um, Santa?" Juniper said. "The portal—the one just outside? It's already closed!"

Santa smiled. "That's all right—we'll take the scenic route." He stepped to the doorway and whistled.

A second later Chris heard the jingle of bells and the stamping of hooves.

"Come along!" Santa strode outside. "There's room in the sleigh for everyone!"

Chris gasped. "We're riding home in your sleigh?" he cried.

Peppermint Bark was already bounding outside. "You'll love it!" he exclaimed. "It's super fun!" Then he stopped and shot Santa a sheepish look. "Um, I mean, can I ride in the sleigh too?"

"Of course!" Santa strode over to give the little dog a pat. "*This* time . . ."

He paused. Peppermint Bark's tail drooped slightly.

Then Santa let out a loud *ho ho ho!* and added: "And every Christmas from now on!"

They all climbed aboard. There was plenty of room for everyone, since all the gifts had already been distributed to lucky girls and boys all over the world. So Santa invited Mrs. Claus, Happy, and Juniper to ride along too.

"Cool! It's my first time riding in the sleigh!" Happy exclaimed.

"Mine too," Juniper said, sounding a bit awed.

Chris glanced at Mrs. Claus. She just smiled as she

settled into the front seat beside Santa. "Not me," she said.

Juniper gasped. "But nobody rides with Santa on Christmas!" she cried. "Always been that way!"

Mrs. Claus winked at her husband. "Who said anything about Christmas?"

"Ho ho ho," Santa chuckled. "It's true. I mean, we have to keep the reindeer fit somehow, right? What better way than to go for an occasional joy ride with the most wonderful woman at the North Pole?"

Mrs. Claus raised an eyebrow. "I'm the *only* woman at the North Pole," she reminded Santa.

"Hey, what about me?" Juniper protested.

Santa chuckled again and winked at the elf. "I meant human woman, of course," he corrected himself. "And my wife is certainly the most wonderful one of those around here, wouldn't you agree? But that's not all—she's the most wonderful woman in the rest of the world, too."

Chris and the other kids laughed, and Juniper nodded. Happy hardly seemed to have heard the exchange, though. He was leaning out over the edge of the sleigh. "First portals, and now this?" he exclaimed. "Wow, this Christmas is turning out to be quite an adventure!"

"Yeah." Chris looked over at his sister. "It's amazing!"

Soon the sleigh was swooping out through the gates. The reindeer flew right past the spot where the portal had been, across the tundra and over a pack of wolves running across the snow. Chris shivered as he peered down at the pack, glad that he didn't have to live with them for the next year!

Still, he was a little bit sad to be leaving. Peppermint Bark was snuggled right next to him in the sleigh, and Chris couldn't quite believe that he'd have to say goodbye to his new friend very soon . . .

"I'll really miss you, you know," Chris whispered to Santa's puppy, giving him a hug.

"Me too," Peppermint Bark said sadly. "But I'll never forget you."

Just then Santa looked back from the driver's seat. "Don't fret, you two," the jolly old man said. "Now that I've streamlined my Christmas Day journey, I should have a little extra time next year, too. Maybe even enough time for a little visit . . ."

Chris gasped so loudly that Holly and Ivy looked over. "What?" Holly demanded. "What's going on?"

"Did you say something about a visit?" Ivy added.

Santa chuckled. "Absolutely," he said. "Peppermint Bark will be busy for most of Christmas Day helping me here in the sleigh, of course. But once we're finished . . ." He laid a finger aside of his nose and winked. "We might have enough time to swing back through Poinsettia on our way home and pick you guys up."

"You mean we can come back?" Ivy cried.

"Really?" Holly added.

Chris couldn't speak. He just hugged Peppermint Bark harder.

"On one condition," Santa said with a smile. "As long as you three stick together, then yes, you can come back and visit us again next year!"

Mrs. Claus clasped her hands. "Fantastic!" she exclaimed. "If there's time, maybe we can go skiing. I'll lay in some extra cocoa for afterward."

"Hooray!" Peppermint Bark jumped up to lick Chris on the nose. "I'll see you next year, Chris!"

"That's right, buddy." Chris rubbed the little dog's ears, feeling so happy he was afraid his heart might burst out of his chest. Maybe he hadn't been sure about Ivy at first, but somehow, after tonight, she felt like part of the family. He hoped she felt it too—like Chris and Holly were the brother and sister she'd always wanted.

"I can't wait!" he added, smiling at the two girls, who smiled right back.

Santa flicked the reins, steering the reindeer toward another portal flickering on the horizon. "Ho ho ho," he chortled loudly. "There are still a few more minutes left this year, so say it with me . . ."

Chris joined in with the others at the top of his lungs: "MERRY CHRISTMAS!"

. . . AND TO ALL A GOOD NIGHT!